"That's it, boy, g

Curiosity got the b
up to see Gillian an Bud engrossed in a game of fetch. Though the injured dog hobbled, he yelped out a succession of high-pitched, happy barks. The kind Joe hadn't heard him make since he'd been with Joe's daughter, Meggie, whiling away summer afternoons playing tug-of-war on the grassy lawn by the pool.

Gillian's full lips and bright eyes united in one big smile. Her still-wet hair curled about her face. Where it fell to her shoulders, her navy blue T-shirt with the yellow U.S. Marshal logo was damp.

"Good boy...yes, you are a good boy." Bud had brought the stick back and was now reaping his reward—a thorough rubdown and petting.

A flash of jealousy shocked Joe's system.

He wanted Gillian's attention. *He* wanted to be the good boy.

Dear Reader,

Joe and Gillian's story evolved from a magical trip my husband and I took to the West Coast. Earlier that year, I'd gone through some tough personal stuff—long story. My husband had discount flight privileges through the company he worked for, so when vacation time rolled around, he suggested leaving our twins with his family, then heading to Oregon. (After visiting the state's coast years earlier on business, he'd always wanted to go back.)

Anyway, we had no reservations except for our rental car and arrived in Portland in the middle of the night. The next morning we woke to fog so thick it was hard to see your hand in front of your face, let alone drive. Still, we slowly wound our way through thick forests to the Pacific. As in a dream, the fog lifted, and there it was, sparkling and gorgeous.

The tide was low and we walked across a beach strewn with beautiful black stones—many perfectly round like marbles. Next we came to tidal pools. Like the ones on Joe's island, each pool housed an amazing array of life—starfish and anemones and so many fish I couldn't begin to name them.

Farther down the road were giant sea caves, and then quaint little restaurants where we'd split a bowl of chowder. Like Joe, I found the Oregon coast to be an incredible place of healing. From forests thick with ferns and trees taller than many of the buildings we had back home in Oklahoma, to miles of deserted beaches, nature put on such a dazzling show I didn't have time to think of anything but how lucky I was to be alive.

Wish you a lifetime of healing journeys,

Laura Marie Altom

You can reach me through my Web site at www.lauramariealtom.com or write to me at P.O. Box 2074, Tulsa, OK 74101.

SAVING JOE
LAURA MARIE ALTOM

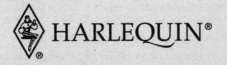

HARLEQUIN®

TORONTO • NEW YORK • LONDON
AMSTERDAM • PARIS • SYDNEY • HAMBURG
STOCKHOLM • ATHENS • TOKYO • MILAN • MADRID
PRAGUE • WARSAW • BUDAPEST • AUCKLAND

ISBN 0-373-75090-0

SAVING JOE

Copyright © 2005 by Laura Marie Altom.

This edition published by arrangement with Harlequin Books S.A.

® and TM are trademarks of the publisher. Trademarks indicated with ® are registered in the United States Patent and Trademark Office, the Canadian Trade Marks Office and in other countries.

www.eHarlequin.com

Printed in U.S.A.

For Aunt Katie and Uncle Paul. Happy sixtieth anniversary!
The two of you are a real-life *Happily Ever After*.
Thanks so much for being an inspiration not only to me,
but to romantics everywhere! I love you!

Books by Laura Marie Altom

HARLEQUIN AMERICAN ROMANCE

Don't miss any of our special offers. Write to us at the
following address for information on our newest releases.

Harlequin Reader Service
U.S.: 3010 Walden Ave., P.O. Box 1325, Buffalo, NY 14269
Canadian: P.O. Box 609, Fort Erie, Ont. L2A 5X3

The United States Marshals Service

Formed in 1789 by President George Washington, the United States Marshals Service is the oldest federal law enforcement agency—and in my mind, one of the most mysterious. They used to carry out death sentences, catch counterfeiters—even take the national census. According to their Web site, "At virtually every significant point over the years where Constitutional principles or the force of law have been challenged, the marshals were there—and they prevailed." Now the agency primarily focuses on fugitive investigation, prisoner/alien transportation, prisoner management, court security and witness security.

No big mystery there, you say? When I started this series, I didn't think so, either. Intending to nail the details, I marched down to my local marshals' office for an afternoon that will stay with me forever.

After learning the agency's history and being briefed on day-to-day operations, it was time to tour. I saw an impressive courtroom and a prisoner holding cell—not a good place to be! Then we went to the garage to see vehicles and bulletproof vests and guns! Sure, I'm an author, but I'm primarily a mom and wife. I bake cookies and find hubby's always-lost belt. Remind my daughter's cheerleading squad which bow to wear. Nothing made the U.S. Marshals Service spring to life for me more than seeing those weapons—and I'm talking serious weapons! And then I glanced at my tour guide and realized that this guy isn't fictional, but uses these guns, puts his very life on the line protecting me and my family and the rest of this city, county and state. I had chills.

When I started digging for information on the Witness Security Program, things really got interesting. Deputy Marshal Rick ever so politely sidestepped my every question. I found out nothing! Not where the base of operations is located, not which marshals are assigned to the program, where/who those marshals report to on a daily basis, what size crews are used, how their shifts were rotated—nothing! After a while, it got to be a game. One it was obvious I'd lose!

Honestly, all this mystery probably makes for better fiction. I don't want to know what really happens. It's probably not half as romantic as the images of these great protectors I've conjured in my mind. Oh—and another bonus to my tour…Deputy Marshal Rick was Harlequin American Romance–hero hot!

Laura Altom

Chapter One

"Mr. Morgan?" Gillian Logue called above the driving rain.

The man she sought stood there at the grumbling surf's edge, staring at an angry North Pacific. Hands tucked deep in his pockets, broad shoulders braced against the wind, he almost didn't look real—more like some mythical sea king surveying all that was rightfully his.

Gillian shivered, hunching deeper into her pathetic excuse for a jacket.

Even in the rain, the place reeked of fish and seaweed and all things *not* on her L.A. beat. They were achingly familiar smells she could try all she liked to pretend didn't dredge up the past, but there was no denying it—it was hard to come home to Oregon. Not that this island was *home,* but the boulder-strewn coastal landscape sure was.

The crashing waves.

The tangy scent of pines flavored with a rich stew of all things living and dead in the sea.

The times she'd played along the shore as a child.

The times she'd cried along the shore as a woman.

Shoot, who was she to judge Joe Morgan?

Yeah, she'd lost a love, and yeah, it'd hurt, but it wasn't like she'd been married to Kent, or they'd had kids. She couldn't even fathom the complexities of Joe Morgan's pain.

Shouldn't want to.

She wasn't on this godforsaken rock to make a new friend. She was here for one simple reason—to do her job.

"Mr. Morgan?" she called again.

He looked over his shoulder and narrowed his eyes, not bothering to shield them from the rain. "Yeah," he finally shouted. "That's me. Mind telling me who you are? What you want?"

The wind slapped strands of her honey-blond hair in Gillian's face. She took a second to brush them away before stepping close enough to hold out her hand. "Hi," she said. "I'm Deputy U.S. Marshal Gillian Logue."

The set of his jaw told her he had no intention of shaking her hand, so she reached into the right hip pocket of her navy windbreaker and pulled out a black leather wallet.

Flipping it open, she flashed him her silver star.

"I asked you a question," he said.

"I heard you." She notched her chin a fraction higher, hoping the slight movement conveyed at least a dozen messages. The loudest of which was that she might be housed in a small package, but she was as tough as any man—especially him. "I'm here on official business. Over a year ago, the drug lord responsible for killing your wife was released on a technicality. Now, we have him back, and we'd like you to testify."

"What?" He put his hand to his forehead.

"The retrial starts in two weeks. Consider yourself subpoenaed."

His brittle laugh didn't do much for her wavering confidence.

"Because of your penchant for vanishing, my superiors thought it best you have an escort to the trial, along with someone to fill you in on current events—at least those pertaining to locking up this lowlife for good. Anyway," she added with a tight laugh, "for the next two weeks, and the duration of the trial, you're stuck with me."

The man she'd studied quite literally for months eyed her long and hard, delivered a lifeless laugh of his own, then turned his back to her and headed down the beach for the trail leading to his cabin.

"Like it or not, Mr. Morgan, I'm staying!" Her throat ached from shouting over the rain. "Shoot, you may even need my protection! If *we* found you, one of Tsun-Chung's henchman could, too!"

He didn't look back.

"Your testimony's vital to the prosecution's case!"

Still, he kept right on walking.

Okay. Two could play this game.

She jogged to catch up, coming within a few feet of him. "If you won't do it for your country, sir, don't you owe it to your daughter to see that the man responsible for her mother's death is put behind bars?"

He stopped, but didn't turn around. His only movement was a slight clenching of his fists.

"Mr. Morgan, sir, I'm here for the duration. We know you're a private man and we respect that, so I've come alone. And again, in regards to your probability for flight—you have lived in fifteen places over the past twenty months—they left me here without a boat."

"But you have a radio, right? A cell phone?" His whole body clenched, and he still wouldn't look at her.

"Um, no, sir."

"Liar. Call yourself a ride. Otherwise, I'll take you back to the mainland." He grinned, but the gesture didn't come close to reaching his eyes. "In these ten-foot swells, should be a fun ride in my skiff."

Wow.

Gillian hadn't figured this assignment would be a cakewalk, but never had she expected to encounter this barely human ice cube. Scrambling after him up the well-worn trail, she tried not to think about what amazing shape the guy was in to keep this harrowing pace on such a steep hill.

Her footfalls fell silent along the pine needle strewn path.

A little too silent.

The place gave her the creeps.

Nostrils flaring from the pungent smell of resin, she glanced over her shoulder, telling herself it was just the eerie gloom raising goose bumps on her arms. The forest of shore pine, red alder and towering western red cedars closed in on her, blocking the afternoon's weakening gray light, reducing the wind's howl to a gentle shush.

Stepping over a branch that'd fallen onto the trail,

hearing the chatter of small stones skipping down the hillside with each misplaced step, returned Gillian to afternoons spent hiking with her brothers. For the most part, lessons in frustration.

Sure, the scenery had been gorgeous, but as overprotective as Caleb, Beau and Adam had been, it was a wonder they hadn't figured out a way to safely stash her in their backpacks. Ever since their mom had died, when she was just eight, they'd treated her like a china doll, preferring she stay close to the house. Her dad shared that preference.

By the time she'd left for college at eighteen, she'd had enough coddling. Enough questions about her every intended move. Enough—

The slam of Joe's cabin door jolted Gillian back into the present. The metallic thwack of a lock rammed home steeled her resolve to see this assignment through to a successful completion.

This time around, *she* was in charge.

Her dad had never been prouder than when all three of his boys graduated with honors from the University of Oregon, then went on to ace U.S. Marshal's Service exams.

How had he reacted when she'd done the same?

I hope this makes you happy, cupcake. But I think your mother wanted you keeping a fine home. Raising lots of chubby babies.

Gillian swallowed the sentimental knot at the back of her throat.

The only *baby* she'd be handling was the overgrown variety who'd just locked himself in his cabin.

Steeling her spine, she marched right on up to the

covered porch, past a rick of neatly stacked firewood, then banged the heel of her hand on a weather-beaten pine door. "Mr. Morgan, open up. We need to talk."

From inside came a halfhearted bark—of the canine variety.

Stepping a few feet to her left, Gillian cupped her hands to a large paned window and peered inside.

A friendly eyed yellow Lab made his way to the door, doggy toenails clacking on the sections of hardwood floor not covered by thick rag rugs.

Joe Morgan was sitting in an exhausted-looking gray armchair. The rest of the cabin's furnishings looked equally weary. The only items in the room offering any cheer were the crystal-framed photos lining the mantel.

She guessed they represented happier times that even accompanied by the glowing fire in the hearth, still weren't enough to offset the permanent chill in Joe Morgan's heart.

Remembering the turn of events that had led the man to this point, Gillian exchanged a fraction of her professional detachment for compassion.

Over the years, she'd told her brothers and father so many times that she didn't need them or any other overbearing, overly concerned men in her life, that she almost believed it. Then came that one shining summer between her junior and senior years of college when she'd learned that no, she didn't *need* a man, but they sure could be fun when they weren't related!

Gillian fell hard for Kent Hawthorne. He was tall, lean, and golden from hours spent in the summer sun. For those all-too-brief three months, she'd fancied herself in love. She'd wondered if maybe she'd fulfill her mother's wish for her daughter to one day marry and raise her own family.

Gazing at Kent from the back end of a canoe as they'd drifted down one of the sleepy portions of the North Umpqua, images of the beautiful babies they would share ebbed and flowed like the cool, green water. Maybe they'd have a daughter, then a son. The girl would have her daddy's dark hair and freckles, while their son would be a honeyed blonde just like her.

They'd go on family outings together, to the zoo and museums, and to leisurely Sunday morning breakfasts at their favorite waterfront café, where all four of them would fight over the best pages of the *Oregonian*.

Just as easily as those images bloomed, along with autumn's first killing frost, they'd died.

Kent was a year older than her.

He hadn't been able to decide whether to apply for graduate school in Oregon, or take a job with a high-paying, high-profile consulting firm out East.

In the end, he'd gone for the job, leaving Gillian behind. She'd retreated back into her beliefs that the whole married-with-2.5-kids routine would never be for her.

Gazing at the images of Joe Morgan's former life, while she couldn't possibly understand the enormity of his loss, brought her own days of mourning to the surface.

Losing her mother at a time when she'd needed her most.

Losing Kent, even though, truth be told, she'd probably never had him at all.

Gillian took a deep breath and turned back to the door.

"Sir," she said, delivering a lighter knock. "Please,

give me a few minutes. I realize you've already been through so much, but—"

Just as she raised her hand to knock again, the heavy door creaked open.

It'd happened so fast, she needed a second to process that she'd been granted access to the cabin's warmth. As for any human warmth, judging by the scowl Joe Morgan still wore now that he'd wound his way back to his chair, that she might never see.

There did seem to be at least one friendly member of the family. From the reading she'd done on Joe, Gillian knew the Lab belonged to his daughter. So what was he doing here when Meghan was back in Beverly Hills with her maternal grandparents?

The big dog sniffed Gillian's feet and knees, then nudged its soft, silky head up under her hand.

"What's your dog's name?" she asked.

"Bud. Stay away from him."

Ignoring Joe's ridiculously harsh request, Gillian knelt before the dog, turning her face when a big, wet doggy-breath-smelling tongue slicked her cheek.

Eyes narrowed, she recalled from time spent absorbing Joe's file that the dog wasn't named Bud, but *Barney*—after the purple dino.

She shot Joe a look, but let the slip go.

"Aren't you a sweetie," she said to the adorable lug. Thank heavens at least one male in the house was friendly!

"I thought you had something to tell me," Joe said, staring into the dancing fire.

"Look." Gillian slipped off her jacket and slung it

over the back of a lumpy beige-plaid couch. "We can either do this the hard way by being nasty to each other, or the easy way by at least trying to be friends."

Joe laughed—sort of. "Oh, you kill my wife, then wanna be my friend?"

"Whoa," Gillian said, hackles raised. "We were all sick over the loss of your wife, but for the record, four damn fine marshals lost their lives in that incident, as well."

The only indication that he'd even heard her was the twitch in his jaw.

Deciding this whole scene needed lightening up, Gillian reached into her jacket pocket and pulled out a Snickers bar. "Here," she said, crossing the twelve or so feet to Joe's chair. "I heard that when you were in the safe house, you were real fond of these."

Gillian offered him the candy.

After accepting it, he looked at her.

He ran his thumb over the smooth brown wrapper. Brought the candy to his nose and deeply inhaled. Was the secret to breaking down his walls as simple as chocolate?

He parked her gift on a side table, then pushed to his feet. "I'm outta here," he said, brushing past her on his way to the door.

Gillian frowned.

Well, shoot. She pocketed the Snickers while launching a new chase. His loss, her gain. No way was she passing on perfectly good chocolate!

WITH BUD BESIDE HIM, Joe jogged the short distance into the forest, then leaned hard against the trunk of a towering pine.

What's wrong with me?

Trembling, he bowed his head, raked his fingers through his hair.

Why couldn't his mouth form the words of blame he so badly needed to speak? Why couldn't he unleash the wrath that'd lived inside him for so long even he wasn't sure where the past ended and the present began?

Then again, was any of this real, or was it the final stage of him going all the way mad?

He heard the creak of the door, even this far from the cabin.

"Joe?" the woman called, her voice eerie and echoing through the drizzle. "Please come back inside. It's cold out here." There was blessed silence, then the crunch of her footfalls. "We don't have to talk about the case. Hell, we can talk sports if you want. I grew up with three brothers, so I know every sport from football to skiing."

Joe winced. Why wouldn't she go away?

It'd been a long time since he'd carried on polite conversation with anyone besides his in-laws and daughter. With anyone else, he kept to the basics. Since his wife's death, since her killer's release, since the relentless surprise attacks on his life that had transformed him into the nomad he was today, Joe had become a stranger even to himself. And the beauty of it was, he didn't care—at least he hadn't before *she'd* shown up.

Something about knowing this marshal was here made him once again accountable. Honor-bound to conform to society's graces. To offer drinks and food. Shelter and warmth. And he hated that—feeling like he had to do what was expected instead of what he wanted, which was to fling the woman off of his island as if she were of no more consequence than a piece of driftwood marring his shore.

From between the pine boughs, Joe saw Bud saunter to the woman's side, nudging his nose up under her hand in an attempt to get himself a pat.

Oh, but she did far more than just pat the dog.

She cupped her hand about the silky portion of his head beside his ear and smoothed her fingers across the same place over and over. That was Joe's favorite spot to rub the dog. The fur there was perfectly smooth, almost downy in its consistency.

The fur was his.

The dog was his.

The island was his.

"If you'd like," the marshal said, "I could make us something to eat. I make mean scrambled eggs."

As if cued, his stomach growled. It'd been hours since his last meal.

"Joe," she said, "I can't even imagine how hard this must be for you. I mean…" She flopped her hands at her sides. "Here you've been, thinking this whole ordeal was over, when yet again it rears its ugly head…."

Over.

Yes.

It was all supposed to be over.

Funny, though, how it didn't feel over when he wanted to hold his daughter so bad he could scream, but didn't dare go near her more than once every couple of months for fear of her meeting the same fate as her mother.

No matter the personal cost, Meggie had been through

enough. It was his duty, as her dad, to protect her—yet he was the source of the potential danger.

"I don't blame you for being angry with me," the woman said, "with all the marshals assigned to your case."

Damn straight.

"But Joe, the fact of the matter is that we need you. *I* need you. I hate this guy as much as you do. He killed four of my best friends." She stepped closer, off the trail and into tall, winter-dulled weeds.

A sudden breeze whipped strands of her hair in her face, making her look softer, prettier, than a female marshal should. And he hated her all over again for that— for looking so vibrant and alive when his wife was—

"I saw your propane fridge, so I'm assuming you have the basics?"

Not knowing—not caring—if she could see him or not, he nodded.

"I'm great at garbage can casseroles, too," she said. "You know, concoctions made out of the stuff in the fridge that should probably just go in the trash, but I'm too cheap to throw out."

She'd passed the tumble of moss-covered boulders at the edge of the clearing. He wanted her to be quiet, but at the same time, found himself straining to catch her next words.

How long had it been since he'd heard anyone's voice, let alone a woman's?

"French toast is another of my specialties, but I'm guessing you probably don't have any syrup."

Confused not by her question, but his need to answer, he said, "No. No syrup."

"That's okay," she said. "Just so happens, I brought my own. We had no idea how you were set for supplies, and since I eat like a lumberjack, I brought plenty of everything."

"Where is it? Your stuff?" he asked, surprising himself with the question.

"Down at the dock. I figured my being here would be enough of a jolt to your system without you catching sight of all of my junk, too."

He nodded, and tucked his hands in his jeans pockets.

"Is that where your radio is?" he asked. "At the dock?"

"I already told you, I don't—"

"And I already told you—you're lying."

She flinched before forcing a smile. "Now, Joe, is that any way to treat a guest who just offered to share her syrup?"

"You're not a guest," he said, tired of her trying to woo him into conversation.

It'd almost worked, too.

Almost.

"Come on," he said, leaving his shelter to meet her halfway through the field. "We'll radio whoever sent you, and tell them you're ready to go home."

Bud bounded toward him.

She squared her shoulders and, as she had down at the beach, stubbornly raised her chin. "You just don't get it, do you? For the next two weeks, this *is* my home."

Chapter Two

In waning daylight and sheets of rain, Gillian pitched her government-issue tent smack-dab in front of Joe's cabin.

She'd hoped he'd take pity on her and let her camp on his couch, but seeing how he hadn't helped her lug so much as one measly can of beans up that rotten hill of his, she didn't figure he'd cave on letting her back inside. At least his patch of grass was more bearable than those creepy woods.

She felt him watching her through the window, and sure enough, when she spun around to send him a jaunty wave and bright smile, acting as if she was having the most fabulous time of her life, he ducked behind the drapes.

Hard to believe she'd actually begged her boss, William Benton, for this assignment, which he'd begrudgingly, ironically, given her mostly because she was a *she*.

William and the other guys around the L.A. office figured because of her gender, Joe Morgan would cut her some slack. Right.

And just think, after having all this fun with tent stakes, she'd get to dig herself a latrine. Oh boy.

She fished a scrunchy from her backpack, securing her dripping hair in a messy ponytail, then got back to work raising her shelter.

She'd always wanted to go camping as a kid, but her brothers had never let her. Part of Kent's charm had been that he loved all things outdoors, meaning she'd gotten to camp and hike to her heart's content. What her brothers and father didn't know was that while she was on those camping trips, she'd also learned to love rock climbing and white-water kayaking!

Two adrenaline rushes she'd never gotten while working the mind-numbing desk job of organizing the statewide California Court Security Officer Program, which she knew was important, but hardly the stuff of cutting-edge thrills. This assignment might be annoying, but it sure beat the heck out of sitting behind her desk.

Tent assembled, Gillian glanced back over her shoulder to see Joe darting behind bedraggled beige drapes yet again.

Bud licked the window.

Gillian smiled.

The cabin door opened and out bounded the dog, licking and wriggling his way into the tent, then promptly collapsing on the sleeping bag she'd just grabbed off the porch to toss inside.

"Why are you doing this?" Joe shouted over the rain.

"What?"

"Oh, come on. Pitching a tent in this weather? Are you trying to make some kind of point?"

"Only that I'm not leaving until it's time to escort you to the trial."

"What if I told you I'd make my own arrangements to get to the trial if only you'd leave?"

"Sorry," she said with another bright smile. "But like I told you, I don't have a radio we could use to tell anyone about a change in plans."

"You and I both know that's a crock," he said, shoving his hands into his pockets.

"Look," she said, "this bickering is accomplishing nothing more than wasting what little remains of my daylight. Now, if you don't mind, I'd like to set up a security perimeter, then grab a bite to eat."

Lips pressed tight, Joe stared at her, shook his head, then closed the cabin door.

Gillian turned to the dog. "I take it you're staying for dinner?"

Bud-Barney thumped his tail against the tent wall.

JOE YANKED THE LIVING ROOM curtains shut with such force, the old rod holding them shuddered.

She wanted to play games? Fine. He'd let her.

She had a radio stashed somewhere, and they both knew it. If she wanted to spend the next two weeks playing Girl Scout in the rain, who was he to stop her?

Who was he? he thought, storming across the room.

The owner of this freakin' island, that's who.

By God, he had a right to his privacy.

He looked up from his rage to catch a glint of light from the kitchen reflecting off the framed photos lining the fireplace mantel.

Sighing, hastily turning away, Joe swallowed bile-tainted shame.

He had a right to privacy just like Willow had a right to justice. Like Meggie had a right to live a normal life, as opposed to being surrounded by bodyguards 24-7.

What if this time, that murdering low life stayed behind bars? Didn't Joe owe it to the memory of his wife and the future of their daughter to at least cooperate with the woman trying to right the wrong of Willow's death?

He leaned both elbows against the wood plank mantel, landing his gaze on the photo not five inches from his face.

Willow with Meggie.

Sunset on Greystone Beach.

His little girl had fallen asleep in her mother's arms after the three of them had been on a long walk. At the time Joe snapped the picture, he'd found the sight of mother and child enchanting. He still did.

Gazing at the image of them, he found it didn't seem real that Willow was gone. The very idea was a bad dream. As if the reason he hadn't seen her in so long was that he'd been away on extended business.

Business. Had it been a drug lord who'd killed his wife, or in essence was it Joe's own fault? If he hadn't been working that Sunday morning…

Bile again rose in his throat.

How many times was he going to ask himself the same unanswerable questions?

The past was gone, but the future…

He dreamed of one day having this nightmare behind him. Of bringing Meggie here to see the island. The sea cave with its hundreds of starfish lining the rocks at low tide. The pine forest with its tumbling boulders and moss and ferns. She'd love it here—his girl.

But what about the new girl in his life? Was she loving it here? Roughing it in the rain?

Joe groaned. If only he knew what to do.

Oh sure, the proper thing would be to invite the woman inside, share a meal, then listen while she briefed him on the upcoming trial. But the truth of the matter was that the past few years had turned him into a head case.

He didn't used to be like this.

Indecisive.

Standoffish.

Downright rude.

He used to be normal—at least by society's definition.

He'd been a successful entrepreneur, having made a fortune for himself and his investors in the import game. He'd owned a fancy house, a Jag, a Mercedes *and* a Hummer, even a vacation home in Cabo. So why, when he'd so diligently followed the rules of success, had tragedy stolen everything he'd loved?

As afternoon faded to night, the question refused to leave his head.

Joe tried passing time without thinking of either the past or his future. But for the life of him, he couldn't remember what he'd ever done before the nosy female marshal arrived. He'd walked the island of course, but now, to get out of the cabin, he'd have to stroll past her tent.

What if when he was passing, she started to talk?

Even worse, what if like earlier, he couldn't stop himself from wanting to listen?

Ditching the idea of taking a stroll, he went to the small galley kitchen to scrounge up a meal.

Did he have a taste for something simple? Soup? Or was he craving a more substantial meal? Jarred spaghetti? Canned ham?

What was *she* having? Those scrambled eggs of hers? French toast swimming in warm, buttery syrup?

The last time he'd eaten French toast he'd been on vacation in Maui with Willow and her parents. Willow had been six months pregnant, and her belly had been a constant source of fascination. He'd loved rubbing it, kissing it, feeding it and the growing girl tucked safely inside.

Needing to shut out the acute pain that usually followed particularly pleasant memories, Joe yanked open the nearest cabinet door.

In a messy parade along the shelves were canned, boxed and dry goods. Soups, chili, pork and beans, macaroni and cheese, pasta in a couple of shapes and sizes.

Finally figuring he was making too big a deal out of what should have been nothing more than a routine chore, he reached for a can of chicken noodle soup and a roll of stale crackers.

After eating his fill, Joe reflexively set the bowl on the floor for Bud to finish, only the dog wasn't there.

Was he still with their supposed protector?

Anger flashed through him. Of all the places Joe had run, this island was the one where he felt most safe. He didn't need or want her here.

He slipped on the hiking boots he kept by the door, and marched outside. A sliver of yellow moon peeked through a break in the fog. The rain had stopped and the wind had lessened, yet the damp air somehow felt wetter in his lungs than it had before.

Folding his arms across his chest, Joe gazed out at the restless sea, refusing to even glance in the tent's direction.

He cupped his hands to his mouth. "Bud! Come here, boy!"

About twenty yards into the dark, Bud barked, then scurried into the woods, hot on the trail of some small rodent. Ordinarily, Joe gave him the run of the island, but nothing about this night was ordinary and he didn't like the idea of his dog wandering off. He wanted Bud close, safe.

Just in case.

Of what? He didn't know. Just in case. For now, that was reason enough.

"Yo, Bud!" Joe's cry fell flat against the fog. "Bud! Come on, boy, get back here!"

The dog barked, but judging from the sound, he'd traveled a good distance in the short time between calls.

"Damn dog," Joe mumbled, stepping off the porch, and—

Whoop! Whoop! Whoop!

He winced, brought his hands to his ears, blocking the electronic racket.

The annoyance was turned off, only to be followed by the even more grating sound of a tent zipper opening, then a sleepy, "Hmm...looks like I caught something." Gillian grinned at him.

Joe groaned. "You've got to be kidding. You put a perimeter alarm around my cabin?"

She shrugged, ran her fingers through sleep-tousled

hair. She'd changed from her jeans, navy T-shirt and jacket into an all black number hugging her curves like porn star long johns. Swallowing hard, Joe looked away.

The woman was a damn nuisance.

"Was there anything in particular you needed?" she asked, all wide-eyed innocence.

"My dog. Seen him?"

"Up to about an hour ago, he was sleeping next to me. I heard rustling outside the tent, got up to check it out, then the next thing I knew, Bud took off, bouncing like a bunny through the weeds."

During the last part of her explanation, she'd done a little hop that—no. No, the below the belt movement hadn't happened. Even if it had, he could ignore it. He'd been on his own for years.

He was a man.

She was a woman.

It wasn't attraction, but an animalistic urge. An urge he'd damn well fight, out of respect for Willow and Meggie.

Damn this woman and his dog.

If this marshal hadn't shown up—Joe still childishly refused to even think her name—if the dog hadn't run off, his mind could have been mercifully blank after having spent the day pressing himself to the edge of his physical endurance.

As it was, after feeling trapped in the cabin all afternoon, he felt edgy, restless, like he'd be up all night searching for sleep that would never come.

Bud barked again.

Though the fog made distance hard to judge, Joe

knew the mutt was on one hell of a romp. Probably he'd reached the far side of the bluff and still hadn't caught whatever he was chasing.

Turning back to the yellow light spilling from the cabin, Joe washed his face with his hands and sighed.

What the hell. One of them might as well get what their heart desired. For Bud, the object of his desire was a rabbit or mouse. For Joe, it was a second chance.

One he knew would never come.

"You okay?" *she* asked.

"Just dandy."

"Wanna hang out? Talk about it?"

"By *it,* I'm assuming you mean my wife and kid?"

"Look, Joe," she said, "I'm not the enemy, I'm your friend. I'm here to help."

"You wanna help?" he said, hating the low menace to his voice, but finding himself incapable of changing it.

She eagerly nodded.

"Then zip yourself back into that tent and don't come out for the next two weeks."

"COLDER THAN A WITCH'S titty out here," Deputy U.S. Marshal Neil Kavorski said to his partner on the boat. He shrugged deeper into his coat, craving strong black coffee, but knowing with this choppy water he didn't stand a chance of keeping it in a mug long enough to drink.

"You say something?" his kid partner asked, lifting his iPod headphone.

Kavorski shook his head.

The kid went back to using two plastic knives as drumsticks against the cabin cruiser's dash.

"This is BS," Kavorski mumbled, reaching for the binoculars. He held them up to his eyes, but in the fog, there was nothing to see.

He wondered if the other team, on the island's south side, was having better luck. Probably not, but then what did it even matter?

He chuckled.

It wasn't like he didn't already know the outcome of this little party.

"Think I'm going to try for some shut-eye," he said to the kid.

"Huh?" Brimmer tossed down his knives to lift both earpieces. Tinny bass leached through.

"I'll be down below. Taking a nap."

"Aye-aye, Skipper."

"Knock that crap off," Kavorski said. "I know I've put on a few pounds, but it's because of the medication."

"Relax, would you?" The kid grinned, reached for a bag of Cheetos. "That was a compliment. The skipper had his act together. Everyone knows Ginger was all into him."

Keeping a white-knuckled grip on the steep stair rails, Kavorski snorted. "You ever think about anything but women?"

"When I'm not thinking about the job. Which reminds me—you catch that look Logue gave me right before we dropped her off? She wants me bad."

"On that note," Kavorski said with another snort, "wake me when she makes her first move."

"Oh, sure. It'll be two weeks before we even see her again."

"Exactly. Meaning come get me when this gig is over."

"Joe, hon, did you already pack Meggie's toothbrush?"

"Um hmm," he murmured, tucking his arms about Willow's waist. Burying his face in her sweet-smelling hair.

She smelled of…of—dammit, he couldn't remember. Why?

Why couldn't he remember such a simple, basic thing as his own wife's smell?

An insistent knock sounded on the cabin door.

Hands rubbing his eyes, Joe was slow to wake, even slower to realize who would be banging on his door in the middle of the night.

"Joe!" More banging. "Open up, I think Bud's hurt!"

Heart pounding, mouth dry, Joe opened the door to see the marshal covered in mud, her hair wild and tangled with pine needles. "I heard him yelp not long after you went back inside, but with all the fog and everything—" She hunched over, bracing her palms on her thighs. "Sorry. Thought I could get him myself, but—"

Joe grabbed for his boots, then a flashlight, heading for the door.

"You'll need a coat, too," she said. "It's chilly."

"I'll be fine." He brushed past her. "You turn off your babysitting toys?"

She fixed him with a hard stare. "Cut me some slack, would you? I'm just doing my job. And yes—all my perimeter alarms are for the moment turned off."

"Thanks."

"You're welcome." She edged in front of him, holding out her own light. "Here, let me lead. It's been awhile since I heard him, but I remember his general direction."

Joe gave her a gentle shove. "I can handle this on my own."

"No way. Not only am I already attached to that adorable, furry mutt, but if anything happens to you, my job's on the line."

He rolled his eyes. "Like anything's going to happen to me. Besides, with all the rain we've had, it's too slick out there for a woman. I don't need you getting hurt, too."

Gillian's blood boiled.

How many times had her brothers pulled this stunt? *You're just a girl. You're not strong enough. You'll hurt yourself.*

"Get this straight." Fists clenched at her sides, Gillian slowly raised her chin. "Until you appear at that trial, Joe Morgan, you're my responsibility."

"And you," he said, stepping into her personal space, "get this straight. I don't want or need your help looking for my dog. If I should happen upon any bad guys hiding behind a rock, then by all means, feel free to jump out, guns blazin'. But unless that happens, leave me alone."

"No, sir…" She wasn't backing down, not one inch. "I will not leave you alone."

Lips tight, he stared at her before taking his coat from the peg beside the door—not because she'd told him to, but because if Bud was hurt, Joe might need it to keep him warm. "If you insist on coming—keep up."

Chapter Three

Without turning to see what her reaction to his harsh words would be, Joe stepped outside, pulling the door shut with a thud behind him.

Five long, golden rectangles of lantern light fell from the cabin's windows to weed-choked ground. Damp, still air that smelled of wood smoke and pine flared his nostrils. Beyond the glow surrounding the house, the woods stood dark, like an impenetrable row of thugs itching for a good fight.

They were in luck, he decided, raising the collar on his leather coat. His fists were already clenched.

"Bud!" he shouted.

Nothing.

No response other than a distant, rhythmic lapping of waves against the shore, at least until the cabin door opened, and his self-appointed *bodyguard* rustled through tall weeds in his direction.

"Damn dog," Joe muttered, flicking off his light. "Should've left you in L.A. Willow's parents would've treated you like a canine king."

Bit by bit, Joe's eyes adjusted to the gray-green blanket of night as by rote he headed down the path that ran beneath the cliffs to the small meadow where Bud could usually be found.

Joe's footsteps fell heavily as he expelled his breaths in white clouds. The slender moon now hung high, giving off just enough light through the fog to create garish shadows that blocked his way.

"Bud!" He cupped his hands to his mouth. "Bud! Come on, boy. Let's go home."

Still no response.

Not a yelp, yip or whimper—out of the dog, or the woman tight on his heels.

Traveled by foot, the roughly five square mile island provided plenty of areas to get lost—especially at night. And for a citified mutt who spent most of his time lounging in front of the fire, Bud had roamed too far from the cabin.

Fighting a rush of panic, Joe quickened his pace, hopping over a gurgling stream that shone silver in the faint moonlight.

Just as he came upon the meadow where Bud often fled to chase butterflies, an owl hooted, its lonely voice only accentuating the silence.

Where was the stupid pooch?

Joe couldn't lose that dog. He couldn't. Bud represented so much more than a mere companion. He was Joe's link to his old life. He'd been Meggie's tearful gift to him the night Joe had made his goodbyes. *"You take 'im, Daddy. Barney'll protect you from the bad guys."*

As if that wasn't reason enough to save the dog, there

was another one, even more pressing. In light of what had happened earlier that evening with the marshal, the dog was now, in a bizarre way, serving as a chaperone— not against Joe's actions, but his thoughts.

Standing close to her back, at the cabin, he'd been acutely aware of not just her vulnerable size, but her barely there perfume evoking the sweetness of candy and sex. She'd awakened his protective streak. Made him squash the urge to finger-comb pine needles from her hair.

"Yo, Bud!" Joe shouted. "Come on, boy!"

When there was still no response, he kept walking, hunching his shoulders against the cold, stumbling over exposed roots and brambles as he tried making sense of the night that was every bit as cloistering as his mixed-up emotions.

Nearing a bluff dotted with small holes that led to sea caves below, Joe remembered how much the dog liked to bark at the occasional sea lion hanging out on the rocks. They'd walked there together at low tide.

At high tide, the caves were a death trap.

To ward off a chill that had nothing to do with the temperature, Joe cupped his hands to his mouth and shouted, "Bud! Answer me! Where are you, you stupid mutt?"

At first, he heard nothing but the crack of waves breaking against an offshore bank of rocks, but then he barely made out what sounded like a whine.

"Barn? That you?"

"Oh no," said a feminine voice from behind him. "Is he hurt?"

"Go away," Joe said. He was scared, and angered by her intrusion.

By the fact that she might smell his fear.

His vulnerability.

Joe heard the whine again, off to his left. Judging by the muted, echoing tone, the dog had fallen. Was the friend his daughter had named Barney, the constant companion Joe had renamed the generic Bud, because he couldn't bear thinking of Meggie every time he muttered the dog's name, lying there hurt? Had he twisted or broken a leg? Crushed a rib? Was he slowly bleeding to death?

Joe took off at a dead run down the snaking path leading to the beach below. Even in full daylight, the route he followed was treacherous. At night, it was a natural minefield.

Rocks loosened beneath Joe's awkward steps, clacking down the hillside. Adrenaline rushed through him.

"Joe!" the marshal cried. "Be careful! You can't help him if you're hurt!"

At the base of the cliff, Joe ran parallel to the shore, sloshing through frigid tidal pools a foot deep or more.

"Bud!" he hollered, approaching the cave. His voice echoed in the eerie stillness. A fog bank hugged the shore, dulling the lap of the surf.

The whine came again, close, but still muffled.

Scrambling into the mouth of the cave, Joe flicked on his flashlight, hollered the dog's name again, then finally saw his glowing eyes. Just as he'd suspected, Bud had fallen into a crevice at the back of the cave. Even from this distance, Joe saw that he wouldn't be able to reach the narrow space where the dog was lodged.

The marshal sloshed through shallow water behind him.

"Damn," he mumbled. The tide was rising, and judging by the algae- and anemone-covered cavern walls, the entire area would soon be underwater.

If he didn't figure out a solution—quick—the dog would die.

"Here, take my light," she said, tucking it in his jacket pocket. "It'll be a tight squeeze, but I'm pretty sure I can get back there."

"Go away," Joe ordered, already heading for Bud. He wasn't sure how, but no matter what, he *would* find a way to save his dog.

"Come on, don't be like this," she murmured, tugging on his jacket sleeve with one of her small, cold hands.

He wanted to handle this on his own. Wanted to tell her to stay away—for good.

Unfortunately, his heart knew better. The sad fact of the matter was, he couldn't handle this alone. The space was too small, his body too big.

He took a deep breath before aiming the flashlight's beam deeper into the cave. "Follow me. It's slick."

She did follow him, without complaint, without concern for her own safety.

He gripped her firmly by her forearm, helping her over slimy rocks where brutally cold water already swirled. The mammoth cavern ate the ineffectual beam of light. Incoming sea slapped the rocks.

"Bud!" he called.

No answer.

"He'll be all right," she said.

"You can't know that."

"No, but I want to believe it, and sometimes that makes all the difference."

That was just the kind of Pollyanna crap he'd have expected from someone like her.

He knew firsthand that sometimes, no matter how hard a person hoped for certain events to happen, people and dogs don't return from the dead. He held the light high, searching again for the red glow of his pet's eyes.

"There," she said, taking hold of the situation by splashing through the water to the rear of the cave, then scrambling over more algae-covered rocks. "Shine the light this way," she cried. "I've nearly reached him."

Joe did as he was told.

"Hey, Bud," she softly crooned. "Remember me? Your new roomie?"

The dog let out a scratchy whimper.

"How is he?" Joe stood frozen to the spot. "Can you get him?"

"Oh…oh, God."

"What? What does that mean?" Though he asked the question, Joe didn't want the answer. Sure, the dog might be alive now, but that could be a temporary thing.

"There's…blood. Everywhere. And his right front leg, from the way he's got it positioned, I…I hope it's not broken."

The dog was going to die.

Cold misery washed through Joe, replacing the blood in his veins with ice. Hadn't he already been through enough?

"Come on, Bud," the marshal said, her voice sounding faraway and gentle, so gentle. "I know it hurts, but you've got to let me get you out of there. That's it," she crooned. "Good boy. Oh, you're gonna kiss me now, are you? Thank you. A girl can never have too many kisses."

Listen to her, rambling on. Give it up, lady, the dog's a goner.

"Great job." Despite his internal warning, she persisted in comforting the dog. "I knew you could do it. Oh, thank you, more kisses, huh? You're a sweetie pie, aren't you? What a good boy. That's it, just a little farther."

Why was she doing this? Teasing him by making him believe the mutt had even a chance at being all right?

As if speaking to a child, she'd lowered her voice to a hypnotic, deceptively seductive tone. Over and over she crooned sweet nothings to the dog, assuring him that he would be fine because she had come to save him. How long had it been since Joe had heard a woman speak like that?

How long had it been since he'd wanted to?

Hot tears sliced the cold in his cheeks, dredging gullies in his fear.

Why couldn't he be anywhere but this stupid cave? In here, the seduction of her strength, her compassion, echoed off the walls and the rocks and the water, filling a small corner of his mind and spirit with the crazy notion that maybe she was right. Maybe everything would be okay. Maybe her words didn't only apply to the dog, but to himself.

"Joe," she cried, "I've got him. I just need your help to pull both of us out."

No. She no more had his dog than he had his sanity.

"Joe, please. Help. The water's rising."

He swallowed hard, willed his legs to move, promised that if she helped see Bud through to safety, he'd cut her some slack.

She'd wedged herself into the crevice, and he set the flashlight on a protruding rock while settling his hands about her hips. While he pulled, she cradled his dog. Bud's blood was smeared on her face and in great dark splotches across her coat. Yet for all the gruesomeness of that image, it contrasted sharply with the brilliance of her smile.

"Whew, thanks," she said. "It was getting a little close in there."

He helped her perch on one of the rocks, thinking the dog seemed ridiculously large in her arms.

"You're smiling," he said, more to himself than her.

"Well, yeah. Bud's pretty banged up, but I don't think that leg's broken, after all. The bleeding was coming from this impressive gash." She parted the fur on the dog's left front leg to show him. A clean cut about five inches long looked crusty with blood. Tangled and matted into the dog's fur were bits of dried algae, leaves and twigs. "I brought a first aid kit. When we get back to the cabin, I'll fix this up. Maybe numb it, then stitch it a couple times. With rest, he should be right as rain."

Her message sounded too good to be true.

"How do you know something's not broken?" he said. "Or bleeding internally? And how would you know how to give a dog stitches?"

Settling her chin companionably atop Bud's head, she cocked her own head and grinned.

The angelic sight took Joe's breath away.

Mussed as she was by the events of the long night, she still looked beautiful.

Wholesome.

Alive. So very alive.

In the dim light, her eyes sparkled. Strands of tousled blond hair clung to her cheeks. "What do you mean, how do I know?"

It took a second to get past his unexpected appraisal of her appearance and remember what their conversation had been about. "The stitches. How would you know how to give the dog stitches? How do you know he doesn't have more serious injuries?"

A cloud passed over her features and he wished he could take back the words. Had he always been such a grouch?

"Give me some credit. As for the stitches, I have had a little first aid training, you know. As for how I know Bud's not more seriously injured…" She shrugged. "I don't know *how* I know. I just do. Something about his eyes. It's a gut feel kind of thing."

And judging by the sincerity in her face, she was telling the truth. She truly didn't know, and he liked that.

Earlier, Joe had vowed that if she helped rescue Bud he would in turn cut her some slack. She'd fulfilled her half of the bargain, so why wasn't at least part of his quivery sense of relief caused by gratitude for her good work? Why did he still feel so empty inside and cold?

"Hello? Earth to Joe." She waved her slender, bloodstained hand in front of his face. "Just because we've got the dog doesn't mean we're out of trouble. Have you seen the rising tide?"

He glanced over his shoulder.

Dark, churning sea choked the cave's mouth. There was no telling if the inky black was inches or feet deep. With the strong currents and frigid water temperature, it'd be crazy to attempt to make it out that night.

"Come on," he said, gently scooping Bud from Gillian's cradled arms. *Gillian.* At the very least, he owed her the simple courtesy of calling her by name.

In the flashlight's dimming glow, fear came alive in her eyes. "We're not going to swim through that, are we?"

"No," he said, already on the move. Leading more by memory than actual sight, he stepped onto the nearest boulder, praying he wouldn't slip on the slick seaweed. He landed with a jolt, and the dog in his arms whimpered. "Sorry, boy. We'll be there soon."

"Be where?" she inquired from behind him, shining the light over his shoulder.

He shouted above the crack of waves against rock. "We're going back to where you found Bud. You can push Bud through the hole he fell through, then climb up yourself." He paused to gauge her reaction to his plan, but she'd stopped.

"What about you?" she asked.

"What about me?"

"You'll never fit through that hole. How are you getting out?"

"I'm not."

"What are you saying?"

"Nothing."

"Joe…" She held out her hands, a feeble attempt to show him the danger of their surroundings. Her one word said it all.

To stay in the cave would be deadly.

He knew it.

She knew it.

"Go on," he said. "I know what I'm doing. I'll be all right."

"The hell you will."

A cold wave slapped Joe's right foot and the numbing water seeped through his boot, wetting his thick wool sock, slithering like an icy vine around his ankle.

"Gillian," Joe said. "You saved my dog and I'm grateful, but if you don't get the both of you out of here soon, you'll be trapped. By getting myself mixed up in that whole drug case thing, I've already taken more lives than I care to admit, and I damn sure won't be held accountable for yours now, as well."

"Your testimony saved lives. Hundreds. Maybe thousands." Dammit if she didn't raise her chin. "I won't leave you."

He looked away from her determined stare. Sighed.

"Up there," she said, in a voice tinged with panic and cold, waving the ever-weakening flashlight toward the rear of the cave. "That looks like a waterline against the rock. I don't think the waves break beyond that point."

Bud whimpered.

"I'll make you a deal," Joe said. "If you take the dog back to the cabin and get him all bandaged and warmed by the fire, then I promise to spend the night in that hole."

She narrowed her eyes.

"You don't believe me? Geez, lady, what gives you the impression I'd want to end it all in a crappy place like this?"

"The truth?" she said, water now swirling about her knees.

"Is there anything else?"

She aimed the light directly into his eyes. "Back there, just a minute ago, when you first told me to leave you here, you were smiling. Sure, it was a faint smile, but a smile nonetheless." She made a leap of faith, jumping across a swirling froth of water and onto the same rock he shared with the dog. "Just a minute ago, Joe Morgan, you offered to save my life. All I'm trying to do is return the favor."

He laughed. "You ever think to ask why I was smiling, instead of jumping to your own wrong conclusions?"

"Okay," she asked. "Why?"

"Because just like I already told you, I feel directly responsible for my wife's death, and though I couldn't save her, I will, by God, save you."

"But *I'm* already saving *you*."

Bud whined.

"Great," Joe said, taking the lead. "Now that we've got that sorted out, how about we launch a joint mission in saving each other?"

Chapter Four

Gillian's only reply was a grunt as she steadied herself against Joe's right shoulder before stepping past him and onto the next rock.

"Hurry," she said a few seconds later, already a good ten feet deeper into the cave.

Shooting her an actual grin, he shook his head. "I'd forgotten how bossy women can be."

"I'm not bossy, just right. This is no time to dilly-dally."

"Do I seriously look like the type to dilly or dally?"

"Why, Mr. Morgan," she teased. "Was that a joke?"

Passing her, he scowled, then pointed to a deep, high crevice. "Shine the light over there."

She did.

"Think we'll all fit?"

"Sure."

A few minutes later, Gillian landed with a thunk on soft sand. The rock walls surrounding her felt cool and dry. A good sign, she figured, in light of the fact that everything else she'd touched that night had been slimy.

Joe knelt to settle the dog beside her, then he, too, found a seat in the sand before shutting off the flashlight.

Never having been a big fan of the dark, Gillian knew this tight, dank space should've thoroughly creeped her out. But somehow, with Joe and Bud beside her, it didn't seem all that bad. More like an adventure than real danger.

And while, before she had felt like a big screwup on her first time in the field, down in this cave Joe had probably never been safer from the bad guys!

She shivered.

"Cold?" he asked.

"A little." But she suspected her tremors had more to do with the fact that she'd come uncomfortably close to blowing her first assignment than anything to do with the cave's chill. With any luck, her fellow marshals would be so busy playing cards, they wouldn't notice she hadn't called in.

Joe said, "Bud's probably all right if you want to take my coat from him."

"Nah. He needs it more than me. Besides, we're squeezed in here so tight, it'd be more trouble than it's worth just trying to get it on."

She thought she might've felt Joe shrug before settling the dog across their laps. By which point they were wedged so close at their shoulders, hips and legs that damp heat fogged between them. Joe's warmth came as a stark contrast to the sharp rock digging into Gillian's other shoulder.

As the water in the cave rose, its pounding smacks against the rocks lessened into deceptively gentle laps.

Was it coming for them? Or had their dry patch of sand told the truth about keeping them safe?

Bud whimpered.

Gillian instinctively reached down to pet him, only her hand collided with Joe's.

He jerked his back.

Thank God. Had he felt it, too? A sort of split-second biochemical hum passing between them?

She rubbed Bud's silky-soft ear, which was much easier than attempting to deal with her sudden uncomfortable awareness of Joe as a man instead of her assignment. Biochemical. That attraction? All science, and nothing else.

No denying Joe was a bona fide hottie.

Which only helped make their current situation all the more uncomfortable. What this awkward mess called for was talk. Lots and lots of talk. From the first day she'd opened Joe's file, she'd found a question burning to be asked. To some, it might seem insensitive, maybe even flip, but to a man who loved his family as much as Joe Morgan, there was something about his recent actions that didn't add up.

She cleared her throat, then went for it. "How come you left Meghan with your wife's parents?"

"What?" Even in the pitch-black cave, Joe's fury was plain to see. He'd tensed his entire body. His leg and arm, which moments earlier had been pliant, were now unyielding stone.

Ack. The question had been brutal, the answer none of her business. So why couldn't she now keep from blurting, "Sorry, but it doesn't make sense. You just leaving her. Seems to me if you wanted to protect her, you'd keep her with you."

"Not that it's any of your business," he said with a deep sigh. "I see her as often as I think it's safe. I call a lot, too. Yeah, I'd like to be with her more, but seeing how, thanks to everyone's favorite drug lord, I'm now your basic danger magnet, in my best parental judgment, the only way she's safe is if I'm gone."

Under the cover of darkness, Gillian rolled her eyes. "That's a crock. What if Tsun-Chung kidnaps her or your in-laws, using them as bait to get to you?"

"Drop it, Mary Sunshine. Believe me, the thought's occurred to me, and it's not one I like to dwell on."

"We could protect all of you."

"Like you did my wife?"

"Odds are, that kind of thing would never happen again."

"Promise?"

Therein lay the problem.

Of course Gillian couldn't promise. And though she had faith in herself and in her co-workers to do their very best, she saw Joe's point. He'd been burned once by the Witness Protection Program. Why would he want to stick his hand back in the fire?

Unable to argue with Joe's logic, she tried being quiet, but the darkness was oppressive. Complete. Reminded her of that creepy forest they'd marched through on the way from Joe's cabin. Even though they were surely safe from any thug types, her internal danger meter sprouted a fresh crop of goose bumps on her arms.

"You might feel better if you chat," she said, itchy to calm her sudden nerves.

"I might feel better? Or you?"

"Okay," she laughed. "You got me. Never been a big fan of the dark."

"I am. It's peaceful."

"It's dangerous. Boring."

"You ever shut up?"

Being constantly around men, Joe's bark didn't phase her. "You always this much fun?"

"Fun? You call being crammed into a freezing cave that smells like dead fish, with a half-dead dog, no food or water, and a woman who talks more than she breathes, *fun?*"

At that, Gillian shook her head. "Have you ever in your whole life looked on the bright side of a situation?"

"Yeah. And then my wife died and nothing in my life has ever been bright again."

Instantly sobered, Gillian swallowed hard. "Bud's gonna be okay. That's bright, isn't it?"

"Sure. Thanks to you." She felt him lean forward, heard him sigh. "Sorry to be such rotten company. I really do owe you for helping my pal, here, but…" Joe stopped talking to rub the scruff on the animal's neck. She knew, not because she could see him, but because her own hand rested on the dog's head. Her fingers tingled from Joe's radiated heat. "…it's just that this is hard for me."

"What?"

"Small talk. Pretending we have anything even remotely in common."

"Oh, I'll bet between us we could come up with something. What'd you think of the last Brad Pitt movie?"

"Didn't see it."

"What's your favorite color?"

"Black."

She made a face. Kind of morose, but she supposed apropos, considering where he'd been emotionally.

"Used to be green," he surprisingly volunteered. "So?

"What?"

"Your favorite color? It's been awhile since I had a polite conversation, but isn't that how it goes? I talk, then you talk?"

"Yeah. I was just thinking about your green."

"What about it?"

"Which one? There are only about a zillion. Kelly green and bamboo. Forest and teal—which is really more of a blue, but—"

"Money green. I used to spend a lot of time worrying about making it. Then, once I had more than I could spend in a lifetime, I worried about keeping it." He rubbed his chin. "I should've spent more time on my wife and kid. Maybe then I wouldn't have been checking out that new warehouse. I would've been home with them, playing a game of Candyland or grilling by the pool."

"What happened to Willow—it wasn't your fault."

"Yeah, it was."

"We'll agree to disagree on that. As for me worrying about keeping money…" Gillian laughed. "I've never had any. Probably wouldn't know what to do with it if I did."

"It's true, you know. That old saying about money

Saving Joe

not buying happiness. I always thought it was a lie, but hell, I've got millions sitting in an L.A. bank. Fat lot of good it's doing me."

"Ever think about going back? You know, back to L.A. to be with Meghan permanently?"

"I thought we weren't going there."

"We're not. Just answer me that one thing."

"Why?"

"Who knows? Because it's dark, and I'm cold and…" She wanted to believe her reasons for being there went beyond just doing her job. That maybe once all of this was over, he'd go get his little girl. Gillian knew what it felt like to lose her mother. The last thing she wished for Meghan was for her to lose her father, too. Swallowing the sudden lump in her throat, she said, "You're right. It's none of my business. Sorry I asked. I won't again."

Intending to keep her word, Gillian turned her attention to food, meaning it was time to wriggle their only snack from her pocket.

"What're you doing?" Joe asked.

"Cooking supper. Hold out your hand."

He did, and she placed something cold, hard, and at the same time soft on his palm. "What is it?" he asked.

"Taste."

He closed his eyes and all but moaned at the incredible sensation of chocolate melting on his tongue. The Snickers she'd brought him. She must've taken it from the side table after he'd gone. "Thanks," he said. "But back at the cabin, I was a jerk about it. You eat it all."

"No way."

After they'd taken a few minutes to eat, Joe steeled himself for Gillian to once again bring up the topic of Meghan, but she surprised him by staying quiet.

Odd. He hadn't expected her to gracefully drop the subject of Meggie any more than he expected the flash of disappointment he felt—almost as if he'd wanted to talk about his daughter. Needed to, only he never gave himself permission. But here, in the dark, beside this slip of a woman…

Never had he been closer to a confessional. Never had he wanted more to confess.

Everything.

His pain. Grief. Anger. Most of all, guilt.

Somewhere along the line, after Willow's death, after the trial, after saying goodbye to his little girl, he'd stopped believing in the whole concept of good. For him, the word didn't exist.

Life sucked.

Period.

What else was there to consider?

But that had been before this whole mess with Bud. That had been before he'd almost lost his only tangible link with his wife and child. Now that Gillian had mentioned it, Bud's still being not only alive, but in reasonably good shape, was a wonderful thing, and dammit, Joe wanted to talk about it.

He looked her way, but found only inky shadows and the warmth of soft feminine curves. Since he couldn't see her, he imagined her, curled on her side in a comfortable position. Cheek resting on her forearm. All that whiskey-blond hair spilling onto the sand. She'd look inviting. Approachable. Like someone he'd be able to talk to. Not at all like the all-business marshal he knew her to be.

Not even in his single days had he met a woman quite like her. In whatever relationship he'd ever been part of, he'd held the indisputable position of power. It wasn't that he'd had to have it that way, it was just how it'd been. Willow had sometimes teased him about being king of his castle, and he was, or at least used to be. Yet with just a few carefully worded sentences, this Gillian had knocked him on his ass—figuratively speaking, seeing how he'd already been there.

This morning, if someone had told him he'd actually be sorry a woman no longer wanted to hear his sad story, he'd have laughed them off the island. But then his relationship with Gillian had been odd from the start— if what they shared could even be called a relationship.

Bud groaned. He lifted his head from Joe's knee, and Joe took the opportunity to stretch.

The dog stood, then circled, landing his butt on Joe and his head on Gillian. For a second, jealousy pricked Joe's gut. The dog was his, so why was he lounging all over this woman? Worse yet, why did Joe care? Come first light, he'd see about getting her off his island and out of his life.

Sure about that?

For the first time since her arrival, no, Joe wasn't sure.

In the darkness, his sense of smell was heightened. Rising above the scents of the sea was her fruity shampoo. He used whatever generic brand the guy he'd hired to stock the place upon his arrival had provided. It smelled like lye. It was a bad smell. One he didn't mind because now that Willow was dead, he wasn't supposed to enjoy any part of his life. Yet even recognizing all of that, he couldn't stop himself from taking another whiff.

Without knowing it, he'd craved human companionship. Maybe if he could explain to someone about his guilt, it'd somehow make it easier to bear. Unfortunately, judging by her slow, metered breaths, he was too late for any more talk tonight. Little Miss Chit-Chat had drifted off to sleep.

"MORNIN', SKIPPER." The kid looked up from the gloppy mess he was making of the last jar of peanut butter.

Kavorski grunted.

"Have a good night's sleep?"

"I've had better rest on a horse than on this boat." Kavorski eased himself into the dinette's too narrow booth. Damn sharp table edge made him feel like a gutted fish.

"Want a sandwich?"

"Thanks. Make it a double."

While the kid took two pieces of white bread from a plastic sack, he asked, "Was Team Two scheduled to be out of range anytime today?"

"Not that I know of. Why?"

He slathered peanut butter on the bread. "Just tried reaching them twenty minutes ago. Got zilch. No radio or cell. Thought I'd wait another twenty, then try again."

Kavorski laughed. "Knowing Wesson and Finch, one's in the head and the other still sleepin'."

"Yeah, you're probably right. With all that fog finally

out of the way, I was hoping for some decent views of our guy." The kid handed him his sandwich.

Kavorski snorted. "Yeah, and I know just what view you were hoping for."

"Ha ha. I already told you, Logue's off-limits for the next two weeks, but after that…" He whistled.

"Quit your daydreaming and give Team Two another call. Then wake up the princess. She's past due for calling in."

"Aye, aye, Skipper."

GILLIAN OPENED HER EYES to a sight so fantastic she almost believed it a dream.

The tide was out and the cave flooded by brilliant light.

Iridescent green anemones clung to the cavern walls. In luminous tidal pools of blue-green water so glassy clear it didn't look real, lived stars. Purple and green. Striped and mottled. There were tiny darting fish and crabs. Barnacles and clams.

When Gillian was a kid, her mom used to take her down to the tidal pools just to poke around. They'd spend hours, always discovering something new.

How long had it been since she'd let herself remember some of the happy times with her mom, and not just the annoying times with her brothers and father?

Gillian eased to her feet, rubbing her aching lower back.

The night had been endless.

What fun did today hold in store?

Cautiously making her way through the cave, watching her footing on algae-covered rocks, and sloshing through shallow water in spots where there was bare sand, she stepped into the glorious light and heat.

Her feet felt permanently cold and wet, as did her clothes, but just one minute of closing her eyes and tipping her face to the sky made everything better. Her navy jacket and jeans captured the sun, trapping it close to her body where, for a brief moment, she imagined it was Kent's broad hands massaging her shoulders and back....

Only the image behind her mind's eye wasn't Kent, but Joe. Dark and brooding. Crushed beside her in inky black so complete she couldn't see her own fingers.

Eyes open wide, she deeply exhaled.

She was tired. Aching and hungry. A shower and nice, hot meal would clear her head of such ridiculous—not to mention inappropriate—thoughts.

From out of nowhere, a cloud of emotion rained behind her eyes, causing her to blink to hold back pending tears.

What was she doing here?

She should've stayed in LA, where it was safe. Not that she feared for her physical safety, but emotionally, coastal Oregon wasn't a good place. When she'd left here, she'd sworn to never come back.

There was a reason Joe Morgan had run off and left his little girl—he was messed up in the head. Just as she soon would be if she didn't keep her wits about her and remember not who she used to be, but who she currently was. She hadn't returned to the shore to dredge up bittersweet memories of her mom or stifling memories of her overprotective father and big brothers, but, plain and simple, to do her job.

Chapter Five

Joe looked out at the seamless Pacific and sadly laughed. Wasn't it just his luck that on the one day he was in the mood for a fierce gale, not a breath of air stirred the sea oats, or even his hair?

He knelt to pick up a smooth black stone, and skipped it over the water. One, twice, three times it hopped before finally sinking. It'd only been that many times, possibly a handful more, that he hadn't dreamed about Willow. Three, maybe four times in all those years. Yet last night it'd happened again.

Squeezing his eyes shut until they stung from the pressure, he willed a certain marshal to vanish from his life and prosper elsewhere. She was ruining everything. Making him think he wanted to talk when all he really wanted was to… There she was, walking along his shore.

Jean hems rolled up. Jacket tied around her waist. Hiking boots hanging by the laces over her right shoulder. Dark blue T-shirt clinging to her curves.

She caught sight of him and half waved. "You

shouldn't be out in the open like this. Especially without me. Could be dangerous."

He shot a look at the vacant sea. "You expecting Rambo to pop out of the water in scuba gear?"

"It could happen."

He snorted.

Bud sledded on his butt down the embankment upon which he'd been chasing small rodents. In his limping flurry, he sent stones clattering, all the while barking his hello.

"Well, good morning to you, too," she said. "Looks like at least one of us got a good night's sleep. You must already be feeling better." She knelt, giving the dog a good rub and a hug. While she inspected the healing gash on his leg, Bud wagged and wriggled to the point where if she didn't knock it off, the dog's rear end would need an alignment.

Joe tried looking away, but Bud yelped, dragging his attention back. Only instead of finding an injured mutt, Joe found Gillian tossing a piece of driftwood for the dog to fetch.

Something about the way she put her whole body and soul into the simple act… The way her toothy smile lit not just her eyes, but her entire face…

Joe stood there, hands in his pockets, utterly incapable of looking anywhere but at her. After he'd spent years living in self-imposed darkness, she was light.

"Bud, no!" she cried out with a laugh, chasing after the dog into the surf, where he'd apparently found something more interesting than a stick. To Joe, she said, "Your dog fancies himself to be a fisherman. I wonder how you teach the hazards of catching crabs?"

Joe dragged in a deep breath.

I'm sorry, Willow. God, I'm sorry.

Gillian's smile pulled him like Bud was pulled to the rabbit family that lived in the fallen fir just beyond the glade where blackberries grew. She waved him over, and Joe stiffened, forcing himself to ignore her, to steel himself to her softness. But it was no use. He was trapped.

Trapped in a fantasy world where the feminine voice catching a ride on clean, crisp, briny-smelling air didn't belong to a woman named Gillian, but Willow. And she was here with him now, with their daughter. And life was good, and—

"What's for breakfast?" the marshal asked.

He wanted to hate her for yet again interrupting one of his fantasies, but couldn't. Her smile was too genuine. Unlike those women who'd come on to him after the trial, she wasn't out to snag a rich, tragic widower, but to do her job.

He shrugged. "I usually have a Pop Tart."

"Which flavor?"

"Cherry."

"Cherry, huh?" She cast him a playful pout. "I've always been a blueberry girl. How about French toast instead? Then I should start briefing you on—would you look at that beauty?" She dipped down to peer into a shallow tidal pool at a brilliant orange star. The water's reflection cast a silvery shimmer across her face and body. "It's so pretty," she said, her voice sounding more like an excited kid than a supposedly hardened marshal.

Gently, with just the tip of her index finger, she stroked the creature, and in doing so broke all illusions Joe might've had of her being childlike when her T-shirt rose. Baring her back. Giving him a glimpse of purple thong panties just above the waistline of her jeans.

Good grief.

He looked away. "Yeah. French toast. Sounds good."

"Great." She was smiling again, while quietly, almost secretly, crouching low, tipping her face to the sun. She closed her eyes and slowed her breaths, trailing just the fingertips of her left hand through the pool's mirrored surface. "Mmm," she said with a quiet sigh. "I thought I hated this place, but I'm thinking it was the people who live here that bugged me, not the actual place."

Eyebrows raised, he asked, "You've been here before? To my island?"

"No. But I grew up in Desolation Point. That's what? Only ten, fifteen miles from here—at least once you get back on dry land."

"Uh-huh."

"That's partially why I was chosen for your case. My familiarity with your location."

"How'd you find me?"

"Lucky break. Want details?"

"Sure. Shoot." They began the long walk back to the cabin.

"My brother's a marshal—well, all three of them are, actually. But the oldest, Caleb, dated this girl from Newport. She lives in Portland now, but used to be a bank teller for *Oregon Coast*. One night before a date, he had a couple things to finish up at his office. Had the girl meet him there, and she happened to see a photo of you on his desk. She said the guy looked familiar. You can pretty much connect the dots from there."

Joe shook his head. "Incredible. I've been to that bank exactly twice, and I get recognized."

"If it makes you feel better, she said you were hot, which was why she'd paid such close attention." Gillian gave him a good-natured nudge. "Really ticked my brother off, how she kept repeating that in interview after interview. I loved that—seeing unflappable Caleb good and ruffled. Thanks."

Joe's only response was a snort.

"If you knew my brother, you'd understand."

Without being rude, how could he make it clear he didn't want to know her, let alone her brother!

"God, sometimes he could be such a tool. Constantly in my business. Drilling me about everything from what I'd had for breakfast to asking if I flossed my teeth. Drove me—"

"Don't you ever shut up?"

She stopped on the dirt trail, staring up at him with a look he couldn't begin to decipher. Was she hurt? Angry? Both? Even if she was, what did he care?

He cared, because as she'd pointed out the previous day, she was here to help nail the bastard responsible for his wife's death. "Sorry," he said, determined to at least try civility if not all-out cordiality.

"It's all right. I was trying again to make small talk. You know, help you feel more at ease, but I guess I went overboard." She shrugged. "This is my first field assignment, so I'm kind of on edge, what with already having flubbed my first night."

"You did okay—hell, more than okay, judging by the fact that my dog's still breathing—and barking." Joe managed a half grin, nodding toward the baying going on somewhere over the next hill.

"Thanks, but still… Considering what you've already been through, I should be more professional and keep my personal woes private."

"No. My past is no excuse for my lousy behavior. I've just become so pessimistic, that I don't know…" He looked away. "Guess I live every day expecting it to be my last."

"Look, I know this is probably easy for me to say, but you've got to stop this downward spiral." She cocked her head, staring up at him with sincere brown eyes. "Back in L.A., you've got a daughter who I'm sure misses you very much. Not to diminish your own grief, but Joe, husbands lose wives every day. Wives lose husbands. Granted, most die of cancer or car wrecks, they don't get gunned down, but it wasn't your fault, any more than it was the fault of the marshals who died trying to protect Willow. And now, for better or worse, the two of us have been thrown together. Until it's over, what do you say? Let's just try making the best of it."

He shrugged.

"What?" she asked in a half sarcastic, half amused tone, thrusting out her chin in an obvious challenge. "Mean Joe Morgan isn't going to fight that suggestion?"

"Know what?"

"What?" A sudden breeze whipped strands of her

hair across her cheeks and eyes. In a movement beautiful in its simplicity, she raised her small hands to brush
it away. Those delicate hands had no business holding
guns or chasing bad guys, yet she'd been the one sent
to protect him. Oh, he didn't believe for a second she
was the only one, but still, suddenly he felt as if he
should be protecting her.

Shaking his head, he said, "I forgot. Anyway—and
I can't believe I'm even saying this—but after last
night, I'm too tired to fight anything. Let's just go
home."

For a split second, he toyed with the idea of offering
her his hand as a sort of peace offering, but then he came
to his senses and shoved the almost traitorous append-
age deep into his jeans pocket.

In companionable silence, the threesome trudged
back to the cabin. Man, woman, dog, all a little sore, a
little sluggish, but none the worse for wear. It'd been a
long night, but in the end, a surprisingly good one.

HOME. HE'D SAID, "Let's go home."

Gillian stood at the big picture window in the cabin's
kitchen, racking her brain for an answer to the question
of why that one simple utterance meant so much. After
all, it wasn't as if Joe had meant going home in the
sense that it was hers, so why the tug on her heart when
the word had hung in the air on the trail between them?

"Need anything else?" he asked. He stood before
two upper cabinets, each hand on the knob of an open
door. The pose emphasized his sheer breadth, the mus-
cular ridges of his shoulders and back. Joe was a big

man. Powerful. Yet for all his physical strength, he was a self-admitted mess inside.

Obviously, he'd never be able to forget what'd happened to his wife, but what would it take for him to at least resume his normal life? Return to L.A.? His daughter?

The few photos Gillian had seen of his little girl broke her heart. The day her grandparents had brought her to the courtroom had been even worse. The prosecution had shown grisly crime scene photos. Meghan's stoic grandparents had whisked her out of the filled-to-capacity courtroom, while Gillian hoped that the girl hadn't understood what the photos had even been about. But she'd known, as had everyone else.

Joe had never once looked away. Hadn't even flinched. He'd just sat there, vacant. Much as he'd been yesterday, when she'd arrived. Gillian had wondered if he'd recognize her from the trial, but at the time, he'd been so out of it, and she'd played such an occasional, peripheral role, that she'd deemed it highly unlikely.

"Gillian?" he asked. "Need anything for the French toast?"

She'd been still staring at his shoulders, and looked away. "Thanks, but, um, I've got everything out in my tent."

"You really planning on bunking out there?"

"Unless you plan on sending me an engraved invitation to bunk with you."

After a second, he said, "Guess it'd be okay. I don't sleep all that much. You take the bed. I'll just crash on the sofa."

"No. I've got my sleeping bag and everything.

Maybe it'd just be best if I stayed outside. That way I can keep a closer eye on things."

"Give it to me straight," he said, closing the cabinet doors before pulling out a chair at the table. "How many other marshals are out there right now watching over me?"

"N-none." God, she was a lousy liar. Kavorski had told her as much when she'd given him her latest report, telling him that start to finish, the evening had been uneventful.

Lips pressed tight, Joe sighed. "Even after last night, that's how it's going to be?"

"I'm sorry. I'm not supposed to—"

His expression turned hard. Like her ridiculous company line was just one more reason he'd stopped believing in all things real and good.

"Okay," she said. "Truth. There's a patrol at the north end of the island and the south—strictly on boats, though. Nobody wants you spooked."

"And the fact that you didn't radio in last night?"

She looked down. "Minimal radio contact unless there's trouble. My boss wants Tsun-Chung bad. Meaning he wants you in the right frame of mind for the trial. Which is why he was willing to go to these kinds of lengths to insure you don't vanish again."

With one hand tucked in his pocket, the other clenching the back of the chair, Joe nodded.

"What're you thinking?" she asked.

"Does it matter?"

To me it does. This all started out as just her first field assignment, but after meeting Joe, talking to him, spending the long, dark night beside him, waking up to all that healing sun… "Yes."

"All right, then, I'm thinking this whole setup is a crock. You all treat me like some kind of schoolgirl— like I'm gonna pee myself at the sight of a gun."

"No, Joe, that's not it at all." She crossed to him, wanting so badly to reach out to him with at least a comforting touch, but was that sort of thing done in the field? Just how close was she supposed to get?

"Right." He sharply looked away.

She stood her ground. "Can you honestly say that given the chance, at the first sight of me—or any other agent—you wouldn't have run?"

Silence.

"But don't you see, Joe? You can't go on hiding any more than you can run again. Tsun-Chung has to be dealt with." As did the other abandoned areas of Joe's life. What was he going to do about Meghan? What would he say when all of a sudden she was graduating from high school and he didn't even know her best friends' names?

Shooting her a bone-chilling look of what she could only guess was disgust, he said, "I'm going for a walk. Is that allowed?"

"Not without me going with you."

"Am I allowed to take a piss by myself, or you wanna be with me then, too?"

"There's no need to be crude. Just let me check out the bathroom first. In your current frame of mind, I wouldn't put it past you to try climbing out a window."

For the longest time, he just stared at her, then

laughed. A first since she'd been on the island. It was a wonderful sound. Deep and throaty. Unpracticed, almost as if it had caught him off guard, too.

"What's so funny?" she asked.

"If you'd seen my bathroom window, you'd know." Sitting down hard on the chair he'd pulled out at the table, he rested his elbows on his knees, cradling his forehead in his hands. "I give up. Just fix me some French toast and I promise to be good."

"This sudden turnaround makes me suspicious." Eyes narrowed, she asked, "You planning to lull me into a false sense of security by swooning over my cooking, then making a run for it once I'm too full to chase you?"

"Not a half-bad plan." He raised his eyebrows. "Think it'd work?"

She shook her head. "I'm small, but speedy."

WHILE GILLIAN MANNED the stove, waiting for the French toast to brown, she was acutely aware of Joe standing beside her.

He took three peaches from a pottery bowl on the counter. Held them under the faucet. As cool water ran over his hands, her fingertips tingled. After turning off the faucet, then drying the fruit with a worn red dishrag, he grasped the peaches with just the right amount of strength to hold them steady while he sliced them. Gillian wondered if he'd hold a woman like that.

Strong, but not crushing?

Swallowing hard, she focused on the toast.

He reached into the cabinet for two plates, then divvied up the slices between them.

The French toast was soon done, and after heating syrup in a small saucepan, then dashing out to her tent for the bag of powdered sugar she'd added to her supplies at the last minute—despite knowing the ribbing she'd get if her fellow marshals ever found out—they finally sat down to eat.

One bite, and Joe was gone.

He closed his eyes and groaned.

Whenever he stayed on the island, his diet mainly consisted of canned goods, and stuff like macaroni and cheese that he could make with canned milk. The wife of the guy who stocked and cleaned the cabin occasionally threw in extras like the peaches. Carl—that was the guy's name—had once said his wife worried about Joe, being all alone out here.

Joe looked up to catch Gillian smiling. "What?"

"You. You finished your plate and all but licked it clean in, like, ten seconds. Hungry?"

"I didn't think I was, but yeah. Guess so."

"Want more?"

It was on the tip of his tongue to say no, but why? What was denying himself the pleasure of one lousy breakfast going to do? After all, it wasn't as if just this meal would make him forget his love for Willow, or his guilt over having been the cause of her death. "Would you mind?"

"Not at all." She cast him another smile, only this one was more of a sliver.

It did something to him.

Made him want to smile, too.

It'd been so long, did he even remember how? He

tried, and found that—duh—he did remember. Not only how to smile, but so much more. "My wife… Willow…"

"Yes?" Even though her meal was only half-eaten, Gillian was back at the stove.

"Well, you might already know this, so if you do, stop me, but I was just going to say she was a magazine editor for a small, L.A.-based lifestyles magazine. They ran a lot of breakfast-brunch recipes, and on Saturday mornings she used to try out them out."

"Lucky you." Gillian beat eggs and canned milk, then dredged thick-sliced wheat bread through it.

"She would've liked this. Maybe used your recipe in the magazine."

"Nah. It's nothing special. Just your standard every-day stuff."

"Yeah, well, thanks."

"You're welcome."

After they'd both eaten seconds, Gillian pushed her chair back and stood before grabbing their plates. "I'm assuming the dishwashing equipment is under the sink in the form of a scrub pad?"

"Let me," he said, standing as well. "You cooked." He reached for the plates and, in the process, brushed his fingers against hers. The sensation hit him like a blow. Sure, he'd spent the whole night beside her, but this was somehow different.

It wasn't an emergency forcing them together, but him wanting them together. It was wrong, but felt right. Maybe.

The truth was, he wasn't sure how it felt.

If he should even be wondering how it felt.

The woman was here to do a job. She wasn't here to be his friend, cook or housekeeper.

It sounded simple enough, but nothing about this whole situation was simple. Aside from coming to grips with the loss of his wife—and for all practical reasons, his daughter—having Gillian in his house was probably one of the hardest things he'd ever done.

Chapter Six

Kavorski checked again to make sure the kid was sleeping, then headed out on the deck to radio Team Two's leader, his pal and fellow deputy marshal, Allan Wesson.

As cold as it had been the day before, today was hot. The sea was dead calm.

At first, all that came over the radio was a whole lot of static, but then a scratchy voice said, "Kavorski, that you?"

"Who else you expecting?"

"That nosy kid. When you gonna off him? I cleaned house last night."

"His time's coming. Finch give you any trouble?"

"Nah. But then you know me. I'm not the creative type. Just point and shoot."

"Good. Where're you now?"

"I've set up camp just outside the cozy couple's cabin. Can you believe that stupid bitch is cookin' him breakfast?"

Kavorski laughed. "You're still pissed over her beating you at last year's physicals."

"The hell I am. Just can't stand the thought of having her on my planet another thirteen days."

"Maybe we'll make it twelve. What the boss doesn't know won't hurt him."

Kavorski turned off the radio and smiled.

TWO DAYS LATER, Joe stepped off the back porch and released a long, slow breath.

The generator chugged along, belching out diesel fumes.

He'd grown accustomed to taking cold showers, but after Gillian had cooked him yet another fantastic breakfast, then laid off her talk of the upcoming trial long enough to let him eat in peace, he'd found himself in a charitable mood—even going so far as to offer to fire up the generator so she could take a hot shower.

She was in there now.

He heard her humming through the small slat window. If he closed his eyes, he'd see her. Standing beneath the water's spray. Naked. Curves soap slick. And so he made a point to keep his eyes open until hearing the all-clear signal of the water being turned off.

Why did everything all of a sudden feel so different? The sky was the same fathomless blue. The soaring fir forest just beyond the cabin stood as uncompromising as ever. Everything about his little world was the same. *Or was it?*

He clenched his jaw, still struggling with the image of her raising one of her legs onto the side of the tub to dry it. Running one of his utilitarian white towels over and around her slender calf. Up and around her inner thigh. Through a nest of curls and higher still to her flat stomach that'd have maybe just the barest hint of a curve before sweeping its way to her waist and—no.

Fighting the vision, he stormed to the shed to cut the generator, on his way dragging in a breath of caustic diesel smoke.

The part of him who still remembered bits of Psych 101 rationalized what was happening. Yeah, he still dearly loved his wife. But it'd been over two years since he'd been with her. Simple logic told him the only reason he was having these thoughts about Gillian was because she was female and alive and most importantly—there.

Hell, he'd probably have fantasies like this about Carl's homely teenaged daughter.

But did he?

No.

And not just because she was only seventeen, but because he didn't like girls, he liked women. Independent-thinking, big-breasted— God, there he was, at it again.

He'd hoped the generator's noise would squelch the unbalanced feeling that had begun around about the time he'd caught Gillian carefully dusting Meggie and Willow's pictures on the mantel. And then she'd gone and picked a wildflower bouquet to grace the center of the kitchen table. She'd picked another for the battered coffee table—and suddenly it didn't look so battered anymore. Then she threw a colorful old afghan that'd been included in the cabin's purchase price across one arm of the beat-up sofa.

Through all of this, she'd relayed pertinent details

about the trial, but never once had she made them feel force-fed. They were like natural extensions of their conversations.

And more than anything she'd done for his home, he was thankful to her for that. For letting him make peace with this whole ugly situation in his own way and in his own time.

Bud limped around the side of the shed, tongue hanging, tail wagging.

"Hey, boy," Joe said.

"Whew, that feels better."

Just the sound of Gillian's voice changed him in subtle, primal ways. He stood taller. Strained to catch her every word. Both of those actions were uncalled for, but dammit, he couldn't stop.

"During all of our recent adventures, I think my hair must've soaked up half the salt in the Pacific."

"That so?" He made a point not to look up as he headed back into the shed. Not that he had a reason to go back there, but then he didn't really need one. He *had* to avoid her.

These feelings…

The anticipation brewing every time she stepped into view…

It was no good. Not that he was afraid of loving Willow any less because of her, but because once Gillian left—and she *would* leave—then what was he going to do? He couldn't be lulled into a false sense of security.

"Is something wrong, Joe?" Her voice was laced with concern. "You don't sound like yourself. Is that scratch on your cheek still bothering you?" Yesterday, while out gathering kindling, he'd nicked it on a low-hanging branch.

She followed him into the shed, and in the close, confined space, he smelled the familiar scent of his shampoo, made exotic by the fact that he was smelling it on her. On him, the scent was just soapy. Lye. On her, it'd become exotic. Why couldn't she have just used her own shampoo?

"No," he said, "the scratch is fine." To get away from her, he walked the few steps to where the previous cabin owner had left yard tools hanging on wall-mounted brackets. He reached for a well-worn scythe. The weeds around the cabin were taller than the dog.

He brushed past her, trying his damnedest to ignore the shots of awareness that'd rung through him when their shoulders touched.

"Want me to help? We could go over a few more points on the trial." She trailed after him into bright sunlight.

"Nope. It's a one-man job."

"Okay. Guess me and Bud'll just sit out here and watch."

"Suit yourself." Walking at a brisk pace to the far side of the cabin, he put all his frustration and pent-up energy into whacking the grass. The blade was dull and he had to work extra hard to cut as wide a swath as he liked.

"That's it, boy, go get it!"

Curiosity got the better of Joe and he looked up to see Gillian and Bud engrossed in a game of fetch. Though the injured dog hobbled instead of his usual running, he yelped out a succession of high-pitched happy barks. The kind Joe hadn't heard him make since he'd been with Meggie, wiling away summer afternoons playing tug-of-war on the grassy lawn by the pool.

Gillian's full lips and bright eyes united in one big smile. Her still-wet hair curled about her face. Where it fell to her shoulders, her navy-blue T-shirt with the yellow U.S. Marshal logo was damp.

The shirt was big enough to allow her to fashion a halter of sorts that she tied just below her breasts. On Willow, the top would have been obscene, but Gillian's build was so slight that only a narrow strip of bare skin showed above faded jeans. No marshal he'd ever seen wore that kind of getup. Was this part of her being so new to the work that she hadn't yet learned proper protocol? Or was this a deliberate ploy to help put him at ease?

"Good boy…yes, you are a good boy." Bud had brought the stick back and was now reaping his reward—a thorough rubdown and petting.

A flash of jealousy shocked Joe's system.

He wanted Gillian's attention. He wanted to be the *good boy*. But then how could he ever again be good when the very fact that he was attracted to her made him *bad?*

"Hey, Joe!" she hollered. "Bud must already be feeling better. Look at him go."

Joe pretended not to hear, instead focusing on his chore. The weeds were badly overgrown. This job had to be done. Right away. It was an urgent, urgent undertaking. One that would require all his physical strength and hopefully drain his emotions.

Bud's antics brought Gillian closer. "Wouldn't this

be a great day for a picnic?" she asked while the dog was off retrieving.

"I don't do picnics."

"What do you mean, you *don't do picnics?* Everybody loves a good picnic." She dragged in a deep breath. "Smell the air out here. It's like one of those mountain fresh laundry detergent ads come to life."

"Yeah." *Thwack.* The weeds directly in front of him got it really good.

Bud dropped his stick at Gillian's feet.

She patted the panting dog's head, then threw the stick deep into the forest undergrowth. "You've got to eat lunch, don't you?"

"Yep," Joe said without missing a beat in his slicing and dicing. "Inside, at the table. I'll pop open a can of tuna. You can have a can, too."

"Oh, don't be such a grouch. If I agree to cook it and pack it and haul it, then will you go? On the picnic?"

"Woman…" With the long sleeve of his denim shirt, Joe soaked sweat from his forehead. "What's it gonna take for you to understand I've got better things to do than sit around in the grass gabbing? Look at this place," he said, gesturing to the cabin and its overgrown yard. "This break in the weather could be put to much better use than pleasure."

She frowned. "What kind of attitude is that? Lord knows after what you've been through, Joe, you deserve a little pleasure—even if it is just in the form of a low-key picnic lunch."

As much as Joe wanted to lash out at Gillian for her optimism, looking at her standing there, so pretty with strands of her drying hair being fingered by the warm breeze, he couldn't fault her for having such an idealistic view of the world. Not when he wanted to share that view with her.

He wanted to once again find pleasure in small things. Like a shared meal with a friend. But then maybe sharing a meal under the sky with someone you could really relate to wasn't such a small thing, after all.

Maybe that was everything.

For all he knew, a boatload of Tsun-Chung's hired guns could show up tomorrow.

This one, heart-stoppingly beautiful afternoon might be all he had left to share with the first woman—no, make that the first person—who'd actually made him think about there being a tomorrow. For that monumental good deed, the least he could do was grant her this one small wish.

"Tell you what," he said. "You grab a few leftover breakfast muffins, fix a couple PB and Js and I'll round up a blanket and drinks. Sound like a plan?"

"Yeah," she said. "A good one." Her easy smile did funny things to his stomach that he didn't want to over analyze, but instead, selfishly enjoy.

GILLIAN HAD JUST FINISHED making two sandwiches when she froze. Along with eggs for breakfast, she'd made a batch of box-mix blueberry muffins. There'd been an even dozen.

She'd eaten one. Bud, one. Joe, three.

She'd put the remaining seven in a pretty clay bowl she'd then set in the center of the kitchen table.

The bowl was now empty.

Bud? He'd been pretty energized during their game of fetch.

Joe was rummaging in the closet for the blankets.

"Joe?" she called out.

"Yeah?"

"Did you eat the rest of the muffins?"

"I'm still stuffed from my first round. Why?"

"No reason," she said, glancing over her shoulder. Had to be the dog who ate them. Had to be. Because if Bud hadn't eaten them, that only left…

She swallowed hard, then, just to be safe, slipped off to put her gun and radio in a side pocket of the backpack where she'd stashed their lunch.

"WELL?" Gillian asked three hours later. So far, the day had been idyllic, utterly uneventful as far as her job was concerned, leading her to the conclusion that Bud had indeed been behind the missing muffin mystery. Resting on her elbow with her head propped in her palm, she leaned forward to snag another cracker. "You can't leave me hanging. What happened after Willow backed out of the house deal? Were you mad?"

"Nah," Joe said without a moment's hesitation. "And you know, back then, losing that thousand bucks earnest money was a big deal. Hell, I still remembered what the days of eating only Spaghettios were like. But I guess the one thing that'd always been more important to me than making money was making Willow and our little girl happy."

Not knowing how to respond, Gillian just nodded,

then nibbled the cracker. What would it be like to be loved to such a degree?

While Joe fully reclined on the red plaid blanket, crossing his arms behind his head, she abruptly sat up.

Where only moments earlier she'd felt indescribably content, she now felt restless. Was it all of Joe's stories about his family that'd made her so blue? So full of longing for what she didn't even know?

She finally had a decent job assignment, so why now have regrets for what might have been with Kent? Or even worse, what she might've given up by choosing to follow her brothers' paths just to spite her dad. And was that what she'd done? Abandoned all hope of ever having her own family just because it was what her father wanted—expected—her to do?

From where she and Joe were perched, high atop a rocky, windswept bluff, she could see for miles in all directions. The few scrub oaks and pines hunched from relentless oceanic wind, yet today, all was calm.

A pair of butterflies fluttered around a patch of early wildflowers, and the lonely cry of gulls carried from the shore below. Sun glinted off the windshield of one of her fellow marshals' boats.

While she didn't begrudge Joe his memories, she did envy them. Yeah, she had a few happy times she could remember from her childhood, but beyond that, it seemed as if life had been a constant struggle. Jockeying for favor in her father's eyes, then doing still more jockeying in school and work.

When would she get the okay signal that it was time to relax? To just sit back and enjoy the fruits of her labor?

She glanced at Joe.

He'd closed his eyes, and though she couldn't be sure without closer inspection, it looked as if the barest hint of a contented smile played about the corners of his lips. For the first time since she'd met him, he'd lost that intense mask of rage. Rage at the outside world or rage at himself—she wasn't sure which. Maybe—probably—both. Given more time, what were the odds of him opening up to her? Why did she want him to?

Watching over him was her job.

She wasn't supposed to wonder if he ever thought of her as a friend instead of just as the marshal assigned to protect him. Even worse, she was strictly forbidden to wonder what it might've been like to meet him before he'd met his wife.

In the few taped interviews she'd seen of him before losing his wife, he'd been a completely different man. A sharp dresser wearing custom-tailored charcoal suits or deceptively casual sports clothes. She wanted to know the man who hadn't been rolling in dough. The guy schlepping his books across a rainy college campus. The guy chugging beers at frat parties and cheering on the Lakers.

Indulging in another peek, she found his normally fiercely straight eyebrows softened and gently arched. Her fingertips itched to trace them, to smooth across his deeply tanned forehead and ruddy cheeks. Dark whiskers shadowed his jaws and she wanted to touch them, too.

In just their few days together, she'd formed an odd sort of attachment to the guy. Strictly professional, of course. Probably aided by the fact that before meeting him face-to-face, she'd known him intimately through photos and the details of his file. She knew that while in the safe house, he'd eaten Total every day for breakfast, along with one banana.

Only in her head could she admit she wanted him to be curious about her. She was certainly curious about him. What were his political views? What were his thoughts about the Middle East? The economy?

Most of all, Gillian wanted to know about his wife. The woman he'd loved so much that even though she'd been dead for over two years, his torch for her still burned clear and true.

"Joe?" she asked. "You awake?"

"Mmm-hmm." In her current inquisitive state, she'd take that as a yes.

"How did you propose to Willow?"

If he hadn't been awake already, that question would've done it. Eyes propped half-open and gazing her way, he groaned. "What kind of question is that?"

She shrugged. "No biggie. Just wondering. I mean, you've told me lots about you, Willow and Meggie, but what was your relationship with your wife like before you had your little girl?" *What were you like before earning those frown lines on your forehead?*

Before business or diapers, had he been a flashy romantic, bearing gifts of chocolate and teddy bears? Or more of a closet romantic, bringing Willow one showy bloom plucked fresh from her neighbor's garden? Gillian wanted to know what kind of friend he was. More specifically…what kind of lover. And since she was only wondering all of that in her head, no one—most especially her boss and co-workers—need ever know.

"What can I say…I asked her to marry me."

"Yeah, but…" Gillian shifted on the blanket so they sat face-to-face. "*How* did you ask?"

Grinning, shaking his head, he said, "It was stupid. Really embarrassing cornball stuff."

"So. Let's hear it." Gillian rolled onto her belly, propping her chin on closed fists.

He laughed. "Okay, well, I wanted it to be really special, so I bought this big bouquet."

"What kind of flowers?"

"I don't know," he said. "I couldn't have afforded roses, so it must've been something cheap like carnations or daisies. Anyway, Willow had this mangy old cat she'd found in the alley behind her apartment. She named it Ralph. Ralph liked being fed on a regular basis, but he didn't like being hidden in her bedroom. Seeing how her roommate was allergic to cats and her landlord had rules against pets of any kind—most especially male cats—her bedroom was where he lived. Well, I showed up for our standard Friday night date—knowing full well the roommate from hell had gone home for the weekend—with this massive cheapo bouquet with Willow's microscopic-diamond engagement ring tied to one of the stems. I figured she'd take a big whiff of these flowers, see the ring, then start squealing and crying about how much she wanted to marry me."

"Oh no." Gillian rolled onto her side. "Did her roommate show up and find the cat?"

"Worse. Wanting to make a big impression, I used the spare key I knew Willow kept hidden under this big rock in the front yard. She was all the time locking herself out. Anyway, I used the spare to let myself in ahead of time. Spruce the place up. I popped a gourmet frozen pizza in the oven. Unscrewed a bottle of wine. Lit a candle. Everything was all set when I looked over at the table and saw that damn cat eating the flowers. How it got out of the bedroom, I'm still not sure, but I went to grab the ring, only it wasn't there. Figuring the cat must've bit through the string I'd tied it on with, I looked all over the floor, but couldn't find it. I looked back up and there's Ralph, back on the table, chomping still more flowers. I picked the furball up and started shaking him. You know, not too hard, but hard enough that if he'd eaten Willow's ring, he might cough it up. I mean, geez, I paid, like, a hundred bucks for that ring, and back then, that was a helluva lot of money. Took me six months to save up."

Gillian nodded. "So then did the roommate show up?"

"Worse. Willow walked in on me holding her mangy cat upside down, giving it another shake. Just when she'd really started yelling at me for animal cruelty, Ralph yakked all over the carpet and me and Willow's shoes. I mean, that cat must have thrown up eighteen dozen flowers."

"Did he throw up the ring?"

"Oh, yeah. But by then, Willow was so ticked at me for hurting her cat, she wasn't speaking. Then smoke starts pouring out of the oven from that pizza that'd set me back six bucks. The whole thing's laughable now, but hell, she wouldn't talk to me for a good week. Then I couldn't get my money back on the ring because part of the gold had chipped off."

"Bummer," Gillian said, snatching another cracker. "High quality jewelry does that sometimes."

"Watch it," he warned, landing a playful slug to her shoulder. "Or I just might shake you like that cat."

Grinning, she said, "You'd better watch it. I just might report you for marshal abuse."

They shared a nice, long laugh, then Joe sobered. He put his hand on her shoulder, flooding her with confusion over what his touch was about, then what she wanted his touch to be about. He finally said, "Thanks."

"For what?" She barely heard her voice over her pounding heart. Geez, he'd just cupped his fingers on her shoulder. It was no big deal. So why did the heat flooding her upper body bring a tidal wave of emotion?

Almost as if he'd felt something, too—only he couldn't have because he still cared so much for his wife—he slowly withdrew his hand. "For making me consciously remember good instead of only bad. I mean, I dream about happier times, but try not to blatantly remember."

"Why?"

"Too hard. I'm afraid the pain of it might crush me. But just now…" He shook his head. "I don't know, remembering that crazy night felt good. A couple weeks later—after sanitizing Willow's ring—I tried again, and she said yes. I didn't try any advanced romance techniques, just went for the straight proposal. She squealed and cried and we started kissing and things were really getting good when—"

"Let me guess," Gillian said. "The roommate walked through the door?"

"Worse. Willow's uptight parents."

THAT NIGHT, LONG AFTER Gillian had fallen asleep on Joe's couch—she'd insisted, and he'd been too tired to fight her—he sat at the kitchen table, staring at the calm sea.

He still wasn't sure what to make of the picnic.

The late supper they'd shared of tomato soup and grilled cheese sandwiches had been equally confusing. Gillian had long since told him all he needed to know for the trial, leaving only nice, raw personal stuff to discuss. And like at the picnic that afternoon, Joe had found himself opening up.

This time, it was about Meggie's disastrous third birthday, when the party planning service Willow had hired sent stripping twins instead of Dot's Mobile Petting Zoo.

Joe drank from the glass of water sitting in front of him, chuckling over the memory of Willow's uppercrust mom trying to pretend everything was normal as the twins got good and wound up to a particularly raunchy Prince song.

Seemed like he and Willow had always been running into disasters like that. And back then, it'd all been part of their family charm. God, he'd loved being part of a family.

Where usually the futility of this thought—the knowing he'd never be part of a family again—led his mood straight into the toilet, this time it merely made him wistful, sad and feeling very much alone.

Gillian stirred on the sofa. Chirped a sharp laugh in her sleep. What was she dreaming? Why this sudden urge to know?

Finishing the water, Joe got up to find something to read. He'd thought tonight might be the night he finally found sleep, but he'd been wrong. Tonight was the night he'd only think about sleep…

In between thoughts of her.

He grabbed a book on deep-sea fishing, but instead of finding a seat, he went to the kitchen's big picture window.

It was a clear night. Moonlight shone white on black water. Maybe a quarter mile offshore, a cabin cruiser gently bobbed, dark save for red and green running lights. Gillian's team?

The sight should've given him some measure of peace, but it didn't. Before, when he'd run, he'd done it on his own terms. Now, his life was once again in someone else's hands.

A thump sounded on the front porch, causing Joe to flinch.

Probably just a fallen branch, but unsettling all the same.

"What was that?" asked a sleepy feminine voice from the sofa. Before he could answer, she was up—with a gun.

"Where'd that come from?" he asked. "And why'd you feel the need to sleep with it?"

"Official government business," she said. "And while you tell me what you're still doing up, would you mind stepping away from the window."

"Why?"

"Just do it," Gillian said, still not recovered from the muffin incident. Once he'd abided by her wishes, but not before casting her a dirty look, she took her own peek out the window. Nothing, save for Kavorski's team's boat in the distance. "I'll be back," she said, creeking open the door.

"Where are you going?"

"Just to have a quick look around."

"There something you're not telling me?"

"Like what?"

"Like why all of a sudden you're back in marshal mode?"

"I never left marshal mode. I'm good, huh?" She made sure he was well behind her before unlatching the lock, then slipping into the night, weapon at the ready, damning herself for not having oiled the creaky door.

Outside, her hammering pulse made more noise than the crickets.

On the small porch, a sizable log had fallen from the pile of firewood.

Coincidence?

She set it back on the pile, testing just how hard it would be to topple a log of that size.

Too hard for her to buy that it'd just fallen all on its own. Which meant what, exactly? That she and Joe weren't the only ones on the island? That both teams had allowed some of Tsun-Chung's thugs to slip through and they were now just playing with them? For whatever sick reason allowing them to live just a little while longer?

Queasy, hot and sick all over, Gillian gave the immediate area one last glance, then headed inside.

"Well?" Joe asked.

"All clear," she said with a forced smile. "You should really try getting some rest."

"I will," he said. "Just as soon as you level with me. What made the noise?"

She sighed. "Just a fallen log from the firewood pile. No biggie."

"And that's why you have a white-knuckled grip on your gun?"

She rolled her eyes. "Men. Now, if you'll excuse me, I need to make a trip to the restroom." She bolted the cabin door. Only when she was in the bathroom with its door closed did she turn on the water tap, then reach for the radio she'd earlier stashed under the sink.

"Kavorski?" she said into the mic, as quietly as possible.

"Go ahead."

"We've got trouble."

Chapter Seven

The next night, after finishing the few dishes—Joe had made spaghetti from a jar, so it was her turn to wash up—Gillian crossed the living room, the wood floor chilling the soles of her sock-clad feet. At least they'd match the rest of her, frozen by the idea of sharing more time with Joe, pretending everything was as it should be. Despite Kavorski repeatedly assuring her not a soul could've gotten on the island without one of the two teams seeing them, every nerve in her body told her something wasn't right.

All around her were classic symbols of contentment. A fire, complete with merrily dancing shadows flickering on the walls. An adorable snoozing dog. Sweet smells of wood smoke and an after-dinner pot of coffee. Everything practically screamed, *Be well, be happy, this is a good, safe place.* So why, if all that were true, did she feel with every step closer she came to Joe as if she were stepping through a minefield?

She wanted to tell him about not just the missing muffins and log she suspected had been knocked off the pile by something more than the wind. A part of her—the part growing more fond of Joe by the minute—felt she owed it to him to be honest. The marshal in her told her if she breathed so much as a hint of the truth—whatever it was—Joe would run so fast they might never find him again. Certainly not before the trial, starting in a little under two weeks.

Gillian reached the sofa and sat cross-legged at the end opposite him. Her pose may have been casual, but inside, she remained on alert, ready to pounce.

In the glow of the fire, Gillian studied Joe. The devilish slash of hair over his forehead. His dark gaze, brooding and intense. He was a good man. Exactly the kind of guy she might've picked had she been in the dating market. As it was, she was all about the job. Who had time to date? Perhaps more to the point, who *wanted* to date, knowing her getting hitched would thrill her dad.

It wasn't that she didn't want to make her father happy. It was the principle of the thing. He wanted her brothers to live their lives off in the great, wide world, and her home raising babies. He didn't think she was smart enough or strong enough to hold her current position, but this was the case that would prove her overprotective father and brothers wrong.

That all he is? A case?

Well…

"Willow and I met in college." This statement came out of nowhere. Was he even talking to her?

"Oh?" Gillian said, for lack of anything better to say.

"She was Miss Everything. Sorority queen, head of

the student council, Phi Beta Kappa. When I say she was *everything,* I mean it." His eyes turned glassy. A ghostly smile played about his lips. "Just the sight of her blew me away."

"But, Joe, you're not so—"

"Shh… This isn't about me, but her."

"Okay. Sorry." He seemed to be in a trance. Was he okay?

"Don't be sorry, just let me get this out." He rubbed his forehead. "She was totally out of my league. I come from hardworking, God-fearing folks who never got a damn thing for free. Willow, on the other hand, had an air of expectation about her. I don't know how to describe it other than to say that, her whole life, practically all she'd had to do was want something and it appeared. From ponies to Porsches, furs to fantasy vacations, she'd had it all. She came from a life I could only dream existed. And yet to marry me, she threw it all away. Oh sure, her parents came around to eventually forgive her, but we had a few lean years." He laughed, but the sound, far from being joyful, was heartbreaking. "I took her from imported cheese to macaroni and cheese. From sitting front row center at Broadway plays to sitting on a lumpy old couch watching ninety-nine cent rental movies. We were so broke I couldn't even afford new releases. How could she have ever stuck by me? What had she seen in me?"

Gillian scooted closer to him on the sofa and tentatively placed her hand on his thigh, telling herself to ignore the current she imagined flowed between them. He was foremost, her professional assignment. Second, her friend—but only within the limits her job would allow. "If you ask me," she said softly, "not that you did, only that—"

"What, Gillian? What did she see? I am asking, because for the life of me, I don't know."

"Well, I haven't known you very long." Only the two years she'd studied his file and everything about him, from his favorite foods while in the safe house to the agonized look on his face when he'd left the courthouse the last day of the trial. "But since you're asking, I'd say she thought you were the total package. Smart, funny, full of ambition. You know, the usual stuff girls go for." *Not to mention the fact that you're seriously hot.*

"*Funny,* huh? There's not a damn thing funny about the way I miss my wife and daughter. They mean the world to me…."

"Joe…" Not knowing how to put what needed to be said into kind words, Gillian scooted closer still, moved her hand to his shoulder. "If you wanted, we could get Meghan up here for you tomorrow. But as for Willow, you've got to accept the fact she's gone."

"Don't you think I know?" Where he had been staring into the fire, he now snapped his gaze to hers. "I know it forwards and backwards and sideways and up. What I don't know is how I can ever make up for what I've done with my daughter. Even if all this crap with Tsun-Chung clears up after the trial, what's left? Because of me, she no longer has a mother."

"Would you stop with that? Willow's death was not

your fault. You avoiding Meghan in the name of protecting her is."

The look he cast her was so elemental, so raw with pain, she wished more than anything to take her words back.

If she were brutally honest with herself, maybe she so desperately wanted Joe to move on with his life so he'd see what a great woman sat beside him.

Just thinking such a thing filled Gillian with guilt. But there it was. Out on the table.

She had a thing for Joe Morgan. But as long as that thing never went any further than the confines of her own heart, they'd both be just fine.

"Meghan needs you," she softly said. "Okay, so she might be growing up like some pampered princess with Willow's folks in Beverly Hills, but can you honestly tell me all that money makes up for one hour spent playing catch with you?"

"Why won't you leave me alone?" He planted his hands on her shoulders and squeezed. "What kind of spell do you have over me that makes me want to spill stuff I never—"

"And admit it, Joe, it feels good, doesn't it? Just like when we went on that picnic, it felt good laughing again and—"

"What's with you?" he raged, pushing himself up from the sofa to yank open the front door. "Why won't you mind your own business?"

"You're the one who started this! Remember?"

Too late. He was already out the door.

Where the perimeter alarm went off.

Whoop! Whoop! Whoop!

Bud howled, then scrambled after his master.

Gillian turned off the alarm, then, when Joe was safely out of earshot, radioed an all-clear.

What she didn't tell the guys in the boats circling the island was that while Joe was physically safe, in his head and heart, he was an official mess.

"DAMMIT, WHY ARE YOU following me?" Joe asked an hour later at the windswept bluff where they'd had their picnic.

"It's my job." Standing beside him, Gillian hunkered into her too-thin coat, wishing away the cold, damp wind.

Bud leaned hard against her left leg, and she reached down to rub behind his ears.

High, thin clouds streamed over a crescent moon reflecting light off the windshield of Team One's cabin cruiser. Knowing she wasn't alone should've brought her comfort, but it didn't. Out here in the open, exposed, she felt like a sitting duck. What was the right thing to do in a case like this? Force Joe back to the cabin at gunpoint? He thought he was safe. Kavorski and the rest of the team thought Joe was safe. Why was she the only one who couldn't get past this constant sense of unease?

"I'm sorry I yelled at you."

Because of the wind, Gillian couldn't be sure she'd heard Joe right, but had he actually apologized?

"I shouldn't have gone off on you like that, but dammit, Gillian, I asked you when you first got here to lay off about Meghan, and I mean it. She's sacred. Like some priceless museum artifact that must never be touched. Only admired from a safe distance."

"Give me a break," Gillian said, working hard to hold in a sarcastic snort. "She's a kid. What? You think she's gonna get hurt from a hug? I grew up without my mother, Joe, and I'll tell you what's hurting Meghan most. And that's—"

He spun around and headed back for the cabin.

Bud stayed with her.

Shoulders braced against not only the wind, but the monumental task she'd apparently taken on in trying to convince Joe his little girl needed him, Gillian sighed. The very last thing she wanted to do was spend one more second traipsing after him in the dark, but that was exactly what she did.

HOURS, MAYBE YEARS, LATER, Joe lay in his bed in the darkness, listening to the occasional pop of the fire, to tree limbs scraping the shake-shingle roof, to the sporadic grunts of the dog stretched across the hearth, even to the purely imagined sounds of Gillian's peaceful dreams.

He listened to anything that got his mind off the battle raging in his head. The one where he kicked himself for yet again being such a jerk with Gillian. She hadn't deserved his explosion, so why had it happened? What was it about the woman that brought out the worst in him?

Yeah, he knew it was past time for him to have more contact with Meggie, but what if he screwed her up? Made her as big a head case as he was? Then what? No matter how bad he craved the smells and feel of her little girl softness, there was no way he was putting her at risk.

With Willow's parents, she was safe. Their home had

state-of-the-art security. Whenever she left the house, she had two highly trained bodyguards following her.

What she really needs is her dad.

Deep in his throat, Joe groaned in frustration. There she was again. Gillian, butting into his every thought and action.

For a split second, at the picnic, after he'd told the story of how he'd proposed to Willow, she'd cocked her head just the slightest bit to the left. She usually shoved her long hair into a messy ponytail, but that afternoon, it had been down. Down and long and whiskey-blond and pretty in mellow afternoon sunlight.

That had been the exact moment he'd systematically set about trying to hate her.

How could he have spoken about Willow in one breath, then admired Gillian's hair the next? The whole afternoon had been spoiled.

Even Gillian would agree. And if she wouldn't… well, it didn't matter, because he never planned to tell her.

"Joe?"

After an initial start, he looked toward the couch. "Yeah?"

"You awake?"

"Why?"

"I don't know," she said. "Guess I didn't like how we left things. Seems like I read somewhere it's unhealthy for a relationship when a man and woman go to bed mad."

"That what we have, Gillian? A relationship?" He closed his eyes, heard the sweet whisper of her pushing back the covers, then slipping from her sofa nest. With her every silent footfall, he imagined the floor's chill on the soles of her feet.

He swallowed hard, wishing she'd stayed in her assigned spot. Better yet, in her tent.

He opened his eyes to find her standing before him, backlit by the fading fire's orange glow. Her sleep-tumbled hair looked like a halo, and she wore those damn black porn-star long johns that'd bugged the hell out of him a few nights ago. She was a wisp of a woman. A mere hint of his former wife, so why, why was he compelled to look away from her or else pull her hard against him?

Pure desire, thick and hot and *wrong*, burned in his groin. Forbidden wanting. Traitorous need. Need that in his heart he prayed had nothing to do with her. The way she stood there, staring. The way she licked her lips, sending out an unconscious invitation to kiss.

The two of them were ships drifting upon vastly different seas. His was windswept, roiling turmoil and angst. Hers was calm. Placid, welcoming and warm. Just this one night, he could ease into her waters, selfishly seek comfort in her depths. Just once, he could sneak by the past to catch a glimpse of an unencumbered future.

"Tell me what you're thinking," she quietly asked.

"I can't."

"Yes…yes, you can." She knelt beside the bed, brushing his fevered, unshaven cheek with her cool hand. A shudder rippled through him and he closed his eyes and swallowed. "Why are you doing this?"

The innocent answered his question with a question. "Doing what?"

Joe groaned. Covered his eyes with the heels of his hands.

He felt her still there beside him. Nothing between them but a cushion of heated, supercharged air. He wanted to kiss her like he wanted his next breath. Worse yet, he wanted more. But it wasn't a noble want. Merely a reflection of long-repressed physical needs. He'd be using Gillian. And that was wrong.

"I—I'm sorry," she said. "I don't know what made me come over here. I just felt…"

"That's okay. Me, too. I mean, I'm sorry for earlier." *It's just that I'm changing inside. And it scares me. Ever since you showed up, I've been a mess. Life was simpler alone.*

"You ready to try getting some sleep?" she asked, her voice barely overriding the keening wind.

I might never sleep again. "Sure."

"Yeah, me, too."

Chapter Eight

Bright and early the next morning, Gillian wrinkled her nose. "What are you doing?"

Glancing up from where he knelt on the kitchen floor with a dustpan and broom, Joe said, "What's it look like I'm doing?"

"Duh. I can see you're sweeping, but what made this mess?" What looked like crushed cracker crumbs lined the floor beneath the cabinet hugging the outside wall.

"I woke up hungry, so I thought I'd get a snack, only to open the cabinet and find this." He wagged a tooth-marked wax paper wrapper. Sweeping the last of the mess into the dustpan, he rose to dump it in the under-sink trash. "Hungry mice. One of the many benefits of island living."

"Eeuw. Bud doesn't bark at them?"

"What do you think?" Joe asked, jerking his chin the dog's way. Bud was in his usual spot, curled up on his big, red plaid pillow in front of the hearth, napping. On every other exhalation, he snored.

"Okay, dumb question," Gillian said. "You ever trap them?"

He laughed. "Caught two since you moved in."

She shuddered. "And you didn't tell me?"

"Why?" Eyes crinkled at the corners from the size of his grin, he asked, "Just so you could worry about it?"

"Where do you put their little bodies?"

"I don't kill them. I just catch 'em, then set 'em free in the woods."

"And you've done this with two while I've been here?"

He nodded while getting a wet dishrag from the sink, then wiping out the scene of the nibbling crime.

"And how is it I wasn't with you?"

"You were in the shower or sleeping."

"Okay, what happened to my rule about not leaving my sight?"

"Hey, you want me in the shower with you, I guess that's your call." The minute the words were out, Joe regretted them. Or did he?

Grinning, yet shyly looking away, she'd never looked more pretty to him. She had a morning freshness. Innocence. A kind of intrinsic dewy hope he couldn't help but be drawn to. His initial thought was that the attraction was wrong, but seeing how they'd soon be leaving for the trial—then he'd return here, or head on to one of his other remote hideouts, never to see her again—he supposed a few days living in her light wouldn't do him harm.

"Okay, the shower's one thing," she said, "but while I'm sleeping? How do you manage to skulk around without setting off my alarms?"

He shrugged. "Easy enough to step over now that I know what I'm looking for."

"Wow. You make me feel like one hell of a screwup at my job."

"Don't go getting pouty just 'cause I managed a couple escapes. I came back, didn't I?"

"Yeah, but if I can't even keep you in, how am I supposed to keep the bad guys out?"

"I thought that's what your fellow marshals on the boats were supposed to do?"

"They are, but—"

"You want to do everything on your own—even knock off the bad guys should they arrive?"

Reddening at his uncannily accurate assessment of the situation, Gillian said, "Got a problem with that?" All her life she'd had an overbearing father and three know-it-all brothers trying to do everything for her. This time, she'd once and for all prove she didn't need their help.

"Nope." He crossed his chest. "From here on out, I solemnly swear never to leave your sight—especially when that task involves the shower."

"STAY STILL," Gillian said that afternoon in the cabin's sun-drenched front yard. With their backs safely to the exterior log wall, she had an unencumbered view of their surroundings. On her latest check-in with Kavorski, he'd again reassured her that the mission to protect Joe was a cakewalk. But she felt better remaining alert.

On the beach, seagulls screeched over an early supper. Normally, she would've been dragging the rich blend of conifer and saltwater and damp earth deep into her lungs, but at the moment, the only scent worth noticing was the one she'd learned to associate with the man she'd sworn to protect.

Joe sat in a kitchen chair she'd brought out for the occasion, grumbling with every snip of the scissors. "I still say this whole thing is unnecessary."

"Oh, so you want to show up at your trial looking like Grizzly Adams?" She took a little more off behind his left ear, trying not to notice the warm tinglies climbing the backs of her fingers every time she grazed his warm neck.

Had she been at a five-star hotel, the view of sky and ocean would've set her back a couple of hundred bucks a night, so how come the sight that normally took her breath away now seemed dull in comparison to the fascinating dip at the back of Joe's neck?

"Why can't I get a haircut once we get to town?"

"Because you'll be on lockdown when we get to town."

"Yeah, but what if I look like a dolt with a bowl cut?"

She cleared her throat before stepping around him to enter his line of sight. "Excuse me, but you forget I had three brothers and a dad to practice on. Believe me, I'm way advanced over your average bowl cut."

"Hope so."

She threatened him with the scissors before resuming, only she had to straddle his knee to get to the best cutting angle—definitely not one of her better calls. Still, trying to hold tight to her professionalism, she finished her task, then stepped back to admire the view.

She meant to shoot off something witty and devil-may-care sarcastic, but suddenly found her mouth dry.

Joe had been good-looking before, but with a fresh shave and haircut, he was beyond-belief gorgeous.

"I look okay?"

The moist warmth of his breath fell between them. Was it just the sun's rays that had her so overheated? Joe looked way more than okay. He looked amazing. Amazing enough to have *almost* made her forget she was on the island to do a job—not admire the local wildlife.

"Yeah," she said past a frog in her throat. "Much better. Definitely passable for any court in the nation."

Not to mention any woman!

"QUIT!" GILLIAN SHRIEKED the next morning while struggling to keep Bud in the rusty galvanized tub they were using to give him a bath. "You're getting more soap and water on me than him—and it's cold!"

Because she looked so pretty in dazzling sunshine, with her equally dazzling smile, Joe flicked more suds her way.

Bud barked, lunging to escape, but Gillian held tight. "I think I got the raw end of this deal."

"Oh, like getting my hands in rabbit poop or fish guts or whatever it is he rolled in is fun?"

"He is your dog. I shouldn't be helping at all."

Admiring the way her soaked navy T-shirt hugged her curves, Joe hastily looked away. "I know dog washing isn't in your job description, but thanks for your help."

"You're welcome."

The smile she flashed was different from any he'd previously noted. He'd seen them playful and flirty and sarcastic and sad, but this smile he didn't begin to know how to label, as the sexy-sweet play of her lips didn't quite match up with the wistful melancholy in her eyes.

Joe finished scrubbing Bud's back and hind legs,

then held the dog while Gillian drew fresh water from the hand pump to rinse him, in the process getting way more icy water than necessary on Joe's head. "You did that on purpose," he said, letting Bud go.

Playful smile firmly in place, she flung down the plastic bowl she'd been using. It landed with a clunk on the dirt trail leading alongside the cabin. "What if I did?"

"Then you're gonna pay."

The chase was on.

With Gillian's laugh filling the air, Joe ran after her. But not only was she slippery, she was fast, darting through tall weeds and around boulders like they were some kind of rookie obstacle course.

Once, he thought he'd caught her beneath the pungent-smelling limbs of an extra tall pine, but Bud joined forces with the enemy, getting in the way right when Joe had been going in for a tackle. "Hey, no fair! You can't use my own dog against me."

"What can I say?" With a cocky wink, Gillian said, "I have a way with males of the canine persuasion." And to prove it, she kissed Bud on top of his still-wet head.

The chase was back on, only this time Joe was determined to beat out his dog for a kiss.

He chased and he ran, finally tackling Gillian on a bed of dandelions that looked pretty against her hair.

"You cheated!" Breathless and laughing, she tried squirming out from under him. "Coming after me like that, knowing full well Bud abandoned me to chase a rabbit."

"You know what they say about all being fair in love and war."

"So which is this?" she asked, pupils wide, licking her lips. "Love or war?"

Right before kissing her, he said, "Maybe a little of both."

"NEED HELP?" That night, Joe eased onto the hearth, feeding kindling into a struggling fire.

"No, thanks." Gillian pulled one of her trash can casseroles from the oven.

"We okay?" he asked a few minutes later, while she was scooping the concoction onto their plates. He'd stepped up behind her, pausing just close enough that she knew he was there by his heat.

"About what?"

He cleared his throat, pulled out a chair at the table and sat. "You know. This afternoon. You didn't do a whole lot of police work."

"I'm not a cop." She scooped canned green beans from a saucepan, adding them to their plates.

"You know what I mean."

Yeah. She swallowed hard. She knew exactly what he meant. That afternoon. After washing the dog. After sharing one kiss, then another and another. They'd lazed about in the grass, talking, laughing, dreaming. She'd told him about her hopes of making a professional name for herself. He spoke about making a home for himself and Meghan. About both of them again being safe. He'd taken Gillian's hand, told her that because of people like her, people dedicated to protecting innocent folks from the bad guys, someday that dream would come true.

After that, he'd kissed her some more. And even

though she knew she should be the one strong enough to pull back, she fell deeper into his spell. The spell she'd tried denying, but why?

The sun had been shining.

Her fellow marshals surrounded the island.

If they'd seen anything that could remotely be construed as a danger to Joe, they'd have radioed to tell her. And so she'd lost herself in the moment, the afternoon, the wicked glory of for once in her life indulging in something she knew was wrong, but was powerless to stop.

So when Joe asked if they were okay? No.

She'd never felt less okay. More like ashamed. But at the same time, powerless to stop the affection for him coursing through her.

In a few days, she'd be back in L.A., in a crowded courtroom.

Most likely she and Joe would never spend another moment truly alone. Hopefully, after the trial, he'd go back to his little girl and family. She'd go back to working sixteen-hour days. Save for the memories—like the ones made this perfect afternoon—it'd be over.

And she'd be glad.

Truth be told, her conscience couldn't take much more guilt. What she'd done with him this day, and every other time she'd even fantasized about kissing him, had been wrong.

"Your dinner smells good," he said, taking both their plates and setting them on the table.

She glanced up to see the fire blazing. He was good at building fires. And not just in the hearth.

"Thanks." She wiped her hands on a blue-striped dishrag. "But it's no big deal."

"It is to me."

His simple words warmed her.

Aside from Kent, she'd never had this strange yearning to please a man. At least not a man like Joe. Her father and brothers, yes, but only because she'd been out to prove herself better than them.

With Joe, she found herself caring what he thought, but more because she wanted to help him. In some small way, ease his suffering. She wouldn't fool herself into believing their kisses meant anything more to him than temporarily numbing his pain.

Seated at the table, he took a bite of her concoction. "Tasty. But you never answered my question."

"Which one?"

"We okay? About you feeling like you haven't done enough for me? You have to know that just because we haven't seen any shoot 'em up action, what you've done for me here…" He tapped his index finger against his temple. "It's priceless, Gil. Your friendship. It means a lot."

"I—is that what we are, Joe? Friends?"

"Well, sure. What'd you think?"

She pulled out a chair and joined him.

Truthfully, what she thought was that if they were just friends, he wouldn't have kissed her, held her, as he had. What she thought was that they were playing a game during which he pretended he didn't want to go further with her, and she pretended she didn't feel anything more than casual professional respect for him. But the truth was—

"Nothing," she said, glancing toward the fire to brush away tears. "That's exactly what we are—friends."

"Cool."

"And after the trial, we can send each other Christmas cards for a couple years before forgetting each other altogether."

"I'll never forget you." He scooped up another mouthful of casserole. "You've helped me make a decision long past due."

"Meghan?"

He nodded. "After the trial, I'm going to get her. I'll bring her up here if she wants. Or hell, maybe I'll just stay in L.A. Get back to work."

"That's good, Joe. Real good."

"How about you? Got any plans for after the trial?"

She'd been working on Joe's case for so long, she doubted she could even remember goals she'd had before taking this man on as an assignment. So—what was he?

Friend? Future lover? Potential husband?

He'd become all of the above, while at the same time none of them. What she really wanted for her future was indefinable. Fleeting images of the two of them that would never exist. Must *never* exist. For if they did, she'd have proved her father and brothers right. Not only couldn't she hack it in their world, but from the looks of it, she couldn't even make it in her own.

"No," she said, keeping her gaze locked on the fire. "No plans at all."

"YOU DON'T HAVE TO DO my laundry," Gillian said the next afternoon.

"It's the least I can do." Joe snatched the lone dirty

white sock she'd just fished out from under the bed. "I'd have paid fifty bucks for this haircut back in town. I owe you."

"Still…" She sat on the edge of the bed, eyeing his armful of clothes. "You sure you don't have both of those?"

"What?"

"Socks. I'm missing, like, three pair."

Grinning, he set his current load on the end of the bed, then headed across the room.

"Where are you going?"

"A little place I like to call the black hole for socks." Pausing in front of Bud's bed, he rolled up his sleeves and said, "Watch my back. I'm going in." He tossed aside the dog's smelly quilt, then fished between his pillow and the stone hearth, pulling out three bedraggled white socks. Each looked worse than the one before. All of them were dirt-covered, with the toe portions completely gnawed out. Nike would be embarrassed that their Swoosh logo was still on them.

Nose wrinkled, Gillian said, "Looks like a mouse got ahold of those."

"Yeah. A big mouse who goes by the name of Bud. Wanna try sewing these back up?" he asked, giving them a wag.

"Um, thanks, but he might as well keep 'em. I've got a few more pair."

"You can always borrow some of mine."

"Trying to offset the size of my bill?"

"What bill?"

She winked. "The one I'm going to send for damages done to my wardrobe."

"Whoa, lady. You can't prove it was my dog that did this. The island has a long history of—"

Gillian cleared her throat, then pointed to the open hall door. Bud stood, tail wagging, with another of her Nike socks, this one red, hanging from his mouth. "Care to retract that—" Taking the sock from Bud's mouth, she bit her tongue to keep from screaming.

Chapter Nine

"Kavorski," Gillian hissed into the radio the second Joe stepped into the back hall and stuck his head in the laundry closet. "There's no way in hell that dog could've gotten hold of a bloodied sock by coincidence—especially one of mine."

He laughed into his radio. "Hey, woman, why so antsy? Relax, would you? Say it is blood on that sock, and not paint or ketchup or Kool-Aid. Some fisherman probably cut his hand, used the first thing he could get his hands on to clean the mess, then tossed it in the water. End of story."

Gillian rolled her eyes. "Sir, the odds of that particular style, size and brand of sock randomly ending up on some local fisherman's boat are…" She paused, emitting a frustrated sigh. "Bottom line, your lack of concern for Joe makes me uncomfortable. Might I please speak with Brimmer?"

"No. He's on the crapper. And for the record, might I please remind you who's running this show? How many years seniority do I have on you, Ms. Logue?"

A hot flush crept up her chest and neck. "Thirty, sir."

"That's right. So next time you get a hankering to call me over something this lame—don't."

"Yes, sir."

"And here's another reminder. The guy you're supposed to be protecting is named *Mr.* Morgan—not Joe. Unless, of course, he's become more than just the job to you? And maybe that's why you're all the time calling for backup? You ever heard what happened to the little girl who cried wolf, Ms. Logue?"

"Yes, sir," she said. "It won't happen again, sir."

"See that it doesn't. Over and out."

Trembling all over, Gillian stashed the radio, which she'd been storing in the bathroom cabinet, under one of the kitchen cabinets.

Only then did she dare open her left hand, to the sight that'd prompted her latest bout of panic. No matter what Kavorski said, she knew damn well the stiff, rust-colored substance staining her sock was blood. Now the only question was, whose? And what was she going to do about it?

Hands covering her face, she had to search for her next breath. What was happening to her? On the surface, so many things didn't add up, yet Kavorski, a seasoned professional who'd been competently handling field assignments since she'd been in diapers, implied the only thing wrong with this mission was her overactive imagination.

Fighting tears of frustration she refused to spill, she had to wonder if part of the problem was her undeniable attraction to Joe. He was gorgeous, sweet, silently begging to be coaxed back into the land of the living. Yes, it was wrong, but she wanted to be the one to save him—not just physically, but mentally and spiritually and every other way in between. Which was nuts, because she hardly even knew the guy. She just felt like she knew him because of the hours she'd spent poring over his files.

"Clean socks are on the way."

She jumped. "God, Joe, scare me to death."

"Sorry."

With the compact, stacked washer and drying going, along with the generator, she hadn't heard him. Meaning she wouldn't have been able to hear anyone else approach, either.

"You okay?" he asked. "You seem tense."

"Fine," she said, pasting on a bright smile. "What took you so long?"

"Ran out of soap. Had to run out to the shed."

"Without me? Dammit, Joe, I thought we had an understanding that—"

He clamped his hands around her biceps, destroying her with his proximity. And yes, dammit, his heat. His hold was proprietary. And God help her, she liked it. "What's wrong? Something's changed. You see something? Hear something?"

Yes! "No. Sorry. I didn't get much rest last night."

"You should take the bed."

"Thanks, but I'll be fine. We don't have much longer till…well, you know." Till they left this island to go to trial. Till Joe was back in a safe house, she was back behind her L.A. desk and they never saw each other again.

"WHAT KIND OF STUNT WAS that?" Kavorski said into the radio to Wesson. The kid was down below, gulping split-pea soup like it was filet mignon.

"Which one?"

"Sock? Blood? Ring any bells?"

Wesson chuckled. "Good, huh? Left that sucker right out in the middle of the front yard. That dumb-ass dog thought it was candy. The hour it took me to skin that raccoon, sopping up all that blood, I just imagined it was Logue. God, I hate that bitch."

"I know," Kavorski said. "But for the last time, stay away. There's too much at stake. If we pull this off, we'll leave this island very rich men."

"This is bogus. I could've killed them fifteen times by now."

"Agreed. But we can't afford any screwups. Which is why the boss wants it done at the last minute. We can't afford for anyone at the home office to get suspicious. They've got to think everything's going just as we'd planned. If we do this right, by the time feds catch on, it'll be too late for them to do anything about their star witness being dead. On the other hand, say you shoot Logue or Morgan dead, but the other is just injured and somehow gets away, manages to get to shore, raise an alarm. The boss could find himself in even more hot water than he is now. *Capiche?*"

"Yeah, whatever," Wesson said. "Over and out."

Tucking his radio back in his vest, Wesson reached for his binoculars, then crouched low on the outcropping of rocks overlooking the cabin.

For the moment, both targets were tucked inside. Snug as bugs in a rug.

Wesson spat.

True, he'd be paid a crapload of *dineros* for pulling this off, but the sweetest part of the deal was that he'd have slit Logue's throat for free.

The bitch had jumped ahead of him for promotions, outshone him and the rest of the L.A. crew at yearly physicals. He'd never been all that fond of women. Learned at a young age when his mom would pass out drunk, letting her bastard, mean-drunk boyfriend beat out his frustrations on her kid, that women weren't to be trusted.

Always having loved a good rack, he'd given girls a second chance in high school. Michelle had dumped him for a jock. Kelly had said he was dumb. Heather had said he had too many zits. Chrissy had said they didn't have enough in common.

He'd said they could all go straight to hell.

One of them did, but he'd been too chicken-shit to off the rest. Soon, though, very soon, he'd get the chance to kill again.

And hot damn, but it was going to be a rush.

"CRAP."

Joe glanced up from the same page of *Kon-Tiki* he'd been reading for the past thirty minutes, to see Gillian red-eyed and teary. For the millisecond it took before he spotted the eyedrops in her hand, he'd thought she was upset—about what, he wouldn't have a clue. No way could she be even half as confused as he was over the haircutting incident. Damn, but the woman had turned a usually simple task into a demanding lesson in self-control.

And then there was this afternoon in the kitchen. Something had definitely been bothering her, but what? Something to do with the case? Or him? And if it had been him, what was this urge to do everything in his power to turn her frown back into her usual smile?

"Can I help?" he asked, setting down his book.

"Please. Something in the air's got my allergies going. I never can get the drops in just right." Cross-legged, she scooted deeper into the armchair, resting her head against the back, then scooping her hair out from under it. The pose unwittingly showcased the smooth elegance of her throat. The fullness of her breasts.

An instantaneous, biting hardness seized him, and he took the drops, eager for the excuse to put his mind to the simple task. Only with his fingertips brushing her temples to hold her steady, it was hard to think of anything but her. Her smell. Her softness. "Got it," he said, quickly finishing. "Better?"

She was squeezing her eyes shut and laughing while medicinal-smelling tears oozed from the corners. "If stinging pain could be called *better.* Seriously, though, thanks. Once the initial sting wears off, this stuff usually works pretty good."

He hustled back to his side of the room.

"Kind of leaves me blurry-eyed for a few minutes. Mind reading to me? Or shoot, just talking. Doing something to pass the time."

"Ah, yeah." He picked up his book, grateful for the

distraction. "Want me to start at the beginning? Or just pick up where I left off?"

"Anywhere's fine."

He began to read, and while turning a page, he glanced up to find her settled in the roomy chair, eyes closed. Smiling.

Closing the book, Joe cautiously smiled back.

JOE WOKE TO A STIFF NECK, aching back and a curiously renewed spirit. A quick glance over the back of the sofa showed that the reason for his bolstered mood was still sound asleep—in the bed. Her expression all innocence and peace, Gillian could have been a child, but the tugging at his groin when he focused on her lips proved she was all woman.

A woman who by her own admission was up here solely to do her job and to prove her self-worth to a father and brothers who had apparently drilled it into her that she was just a helpless girl.

Worse yet, Joe's heart belonged to Willow. So where did he get off looking at any part of Gillian—let alone her lips?

And why, in light of that fact, along with knowing that Gillian was fully capable of looking after both of them, did he want nothing more on this cold, gloomy day than to jump out of his temporary bed to stoke the fire, then make his cabin mate a nice hot breakfast? Why did he care that the room's temperature be toasty when she woke?

The mantel clock showed seven, but looking out the windows, Joe figured it could have been any time of day.

A thick fog had rolled in during the night, blanketing the old cabin in a cozy gray mist. Even Bud's internal time clock had been affected by the sky's pallor.

"Need to go outside?" Joe asked the golden-haired mutt.

Without raising his head, Bud thumped his strong tail against the portion of rock hearth his pillow didn't cover.

Joe tossed back the covers and blanched at the frigid morning air. Having been hot from sleeping directly in front of the fire, he'd slipped his T-shirt off sometime during the night. Now, he reached to the sofa arm to pull it on.

Bud danced to the door, so Joe hurried that way, grinning when the second after he'd opened it a mere crack, the dog nosed through, then bolted, already hot on the trail of whatever creature had dared enter his domain.

Too bad he wasn't more concerned about mice.

Joe was closing the door when it occurred to him Gillian's alarm hadn't gone off. But then he remembered her having fallen asleep in her chair.

He'd scooped her up and carried her to the bed, fighting a pang when she snuggled with a sexy little groan into the covers he'd drawn over her.

Now, he looked to the bed, but then hastily turned away.

Sleeping was a private matter. One he shouldn't intrude upon. *Right.* Even as he gave himself the lecture, he couldn't help but again drink in the view.

She hardly took up a third of the big, log-framed bed. Her hair fanned across mounded white pillows. Dark and light. Kind of like the difference in how he'd felt ever since she'd arrived.

With her, instead of focusing on the past, he'd at least been able to step into the present. As for his future… The jury was still out.

Yes, he owed it to Meggie to be a good father, but how was he supposed to do that when most days he didn't even feel like a man? More like an empty shell. She deserved so much more. She loved Willow's parents. They were still reasonably young. Active. She was living a good life.

Good. But were the two of them to make a go at it together, might it be even better? Maybe even great?

What would Willow have wanted him to do?

The answer hit him like a punch in his gut. Willow would want their little girl with him.

But it wasn't that easy.

He'd changed.

Would Meggie even want to be with him all the time instead of just having him be an occasional visitor?

For the first time in a long time, Joe at least wanted to explore the possibility of reclaiming not only his daughter, but his life.

Baby steps. That's what he should take. Get through the trial, then see what came after that.

At the moment, he'd work through breakfast. Then he'd just have to wait and see.

"CORRECT ME IF I'M WRONG here," Gillian said, pushing herself up in bed, "but aren't I supposed to be taking care of you?" She eyed the elaborate breakfast tray with two perfectly fried eggs, hash browns and saucer of canned peaches—they'd finished the last of the fresh ones days earlier. The potatoes' peppery smell was the best thing she'd woke to in a long time. Then she made the mistake of glancing at Joe.

God, he was gorgeous.

She swallowed hard.

"You complaining?" He teased her by taking the tray back.

"No way." She meant to tease him in response, but somehow when her hands landed on his, physical lightning struck, and she snatched them away, back to the safety of her lap. "Thanks, Joe."

"You're welcome." He settled the tray across her knees before returning to the stove.

Gillian had already downed one egg and started on number two when it dawned on her she was in bed instead of the sofa. "Um, Joe?"

"Yeah?" he said over the crackle of his own frying eggs.

"Mind telling me how I ended up between your sheets?"

He told her, and if the food hadn't been so delicious, she'd have lost her appetite. What kind of marshal was she? Rotten. How could she have fallen asleep like that? So soundly she hadn't even woken when Joe carried her to bed? Even worse, how could she have forgotten to set the perimeter alarms? What if something had happened to him? How would she live with herself? With the knowledge that everything her father and brothers thought about her had been right?

"Come on, Gil, don't get all pouty on me. It was an honest mistake. You weren't feeling well. You said your allergies had been bugging you. Everyone has off days."

Hands to her forehead, shaking her head, Gillian said, "Take a second to truly hear what you just said, Joe. Then take another second to remind yourself who I am."

"Yeah, you're a marshal. What of it?"

"What of it?" Setting the tray aside, she shoved back the covers and stood. "I'm here to protect you, only I'm obviously doing a pretty shabby job."

He flipped his eggs. "How so? I'm alive, aren't I?"

"You know what I mean. What if the agents assigned to protect Willow hadn't felt—" She put her hands over her mouth.

"And she died, anyway. What's your point?" His posture changed. From relaxed, his whole body went rigid. His jaw hardened. "Supposedly, the guys watching after her had been at the top of their game. Best of the best. Look what happened."

"Oh, God, Joe. I didn't mean to be so—"

"What? Insensitive? Look." He took the pan off the stove. "Maybe the whole reason I even let you stay here was because you're not like other marshals. And I don't mean that in a bad way."

"But don't you see?" Gillian said. "It *is* bad. I'm supposed to sleep practically sitting up. You know, the whole one-eye-open routine. *Always* on alert. I'm not supposed to be having the best nights' rest of my life. Especially not when—"

"What?"

She'd been about to mention the incidents with the missing muffins and falling log and bloodied sock. But why? Maybe Kavorski had been right, and she was just a hopeless screwup as an agent.

"Gillian? What's wrong?"

She looked down, then back up, smiling. "Nothing. Nothing at all's wrong."

"Good. Then when—and *if*—the time comes when I truly need protecting, you'll be wide-awake and good to go."

Chapter Ten

"You gonna mope all day?" Joe asked over his shoulder after throwing his latest of three dozen perfect casts off the end of the dock.

"You shouldn't be out in the open like this. You're exposed."

"And here I thought you'd be proud of me for trying to catch our supper."

"I've got plenty of dried food. You've got canned goods and pasta and vegetables."

"Yum," he said with a deadpan flourish. "Seriously, Gillian, get over it. You fell asleep. One time. I'm fine. You're fine. I promise not to tell your boss the stupid alarms didn't get set. And hell, with all this fog, how are the bad guys supposed to even find me?"

"Yeah, and with all this fog, if the bad guys did show up, the good guys wouldn't be able to see them in time to stop them. Leaving me alone to protect you, which is why I think we should head back to the cabin."

"We will. Just let me catch dinner first."

She rolled her eyes.

"I saw that. Keep it up, and I won't let you eat any of whatever I catch."

Good. I don't deserve to.

Gillian squared her shoulders, trying to see beyond the fog, but having little luck—not just with uncooperative weather, but the doubts swimming in her head. Were her father and brothers right? Was she not cut out for this job? Did she owe it to Joe to take herself off his case?

Her heart said no, that no one knew him like she did. Cared for him like she did. Her head was only too happy to point out that her heart had no business being involved in any aspect of his case.

A branch cracked somewhere in the forest behind them and she looked that way, only there was nothing to see but swirls of gray. Her stomach tightened.

"If all this scowling is about you feeling like you're not good enough, Gil, think again. Gotta admit, though I was pretty ticked about it at the time, you have a genuine knack for putting folks at ease. Well, guess I shouldn't say *folks* in the plural, seeing how the only people I've ever seen you around is me. But seriously, I'm not sure what kind of head games you played on me—if they were games at all, or just part of your natural charm. But you've got to know that if it hadn't been for you, I never would've even considered testifying on this case. I would've thought it was hopeless. Figured what was the point? That both Meggie and me would be safer if I just stayed put."

"You mean that?"

He cast again. His hook and sinker made a soft plop

when it hit the water. "In the time you've known me, have I struck you as the type to lie?"

"No, but—"

"Hot damn! Got one!"

The excitement over watching Joe reel in a huge sea bass won out over her own fears that she wasn't good enough to do her job. And that cracking branch? Probably just one of the few deer Joe had said were on the island. Not in the mood to stick around and find out, she said, "Seeing how that fish is easily big enough to feed both of us, will you now come with me back to the cabin?"

"I don't know," he said. "Catching this fish was pretty fun. Sure you don't wanna give it a try?"

"Maybe tomorrow."

"All right, then, I suppose you're boss." He shot a charmingly roguish wink her way, causing her stomach to flip.

How was she supposed to think of him in terms of being nothing more than a case when he was pulling stunts like that?

He was obviously placating her. So how come if her father, brothers or guys at the office had pulled the same stunt, she'd have gone ballistic? With Joe, she just felt grateful that he'd finally come to his senses.

"THAT WAS DELICIOUS," Joe said, napkin to his lips. "Had I known you were that good with sea bass, I'd have caught you one days ago."

"Thanks." His unexpected compliment warmed her to her toes. "You forget, this was my backyard, and with four males in the house, there were always plenty of fish to fry."

"Yeah, but I thought they wouldn't let you near a stove?"

"That was only when I was little." She sipped at luke-warm iced tea. "Once I got into my teens, they were all too happy for the kitchen to be my domain. They were real big proponents of women's work and all that." She shrugged. "Guess they probably still are."

"Been awhile since you've seen them?"

"A nice long while. Can't say I miss them."

"Oh, come on." Joe forked up another bite. "Growing up with all that male attention couldn't have been that bad. There had to have been some good times?"

In all fairness, yes, there had been some fun, but that didn't make up for the way her family had made her feel. Like she was *just* a girl.

"Well?"

"Sure there were. I had the most tricked-out pink bike in town. And the best fairy princess bunk bed on the planet—complete with a tower and moat. Trouble was, I didn't want any of that. I wanted baseball bats and Matchbox cars. A regular bike like the boys had. Mine was so girly boys my age laughed at it, and the girls called me a snotty show-off."

"Did you ever try telling your brothers how you felt?"

She shrugged, scooping up a bite of canned green beans. "Wouldn't have done any good."

"And you're the one who's been lecturing me on taking a second chance with my daughter?" Joe raised his eyebrows.

"Touché. Quite a pair, aren't we?" She flashed him a wavery smile.

That what we are, Gillian? A pair?

What a gift that would be. To once again find a friend like he'd had in his wife. But to set the record straight— *just* a friend. Yeah, he was physically attracted to Gillian, but that was just science. She was a good-looking woman. No sense in denying that. But there wasn't more. Couldn't be more.

"Wonder what the weather's supposed to be tomorrow?" She took her last bite of fish.

"Anyone's guess." He took his last bite of beans.

"Yeah."

"Why? Got plans?"

She shrugged. "Might be nice to get out of here for a while. I feel cooped up."

"Thought you said it was safer for me in here?"

"It is." She shot him a look. "But if the weather's okay, I don't see what it'd hurt to take a nice long walk in the woods, where you wouldn't be exposed."

He groaned. "Not another picnic?"

"God forbid." She made a face. "But would it be all right if I happened to stash a chunk of cheese or a candy bar in my pocket? Or do you prefer that your very own personal marshal just starve?"

"Why so testy?" Joe asked.

Gillian looked away.

Gee, could it be she was testy because of his dead silence following her offhand statement calling them a pair? And here he'd had to go and take it all personal, like she'd…like she'd what? Actually thought of the two of them in terms of being a couple?

Absolutely not!

This assignment was wonkers. Way different from any other job her office had handled. Normally, she'd have been on a rotating shift with other teams of marshals. She'd never just be on her own like this. Living with a man. Sharing meals and intimacies such as cooking breakfasts, lunches and dinners. Brushing teeth and helping each other with all sorts of things like applying eyedrops and searching for lost socks.

If it weren't for the bloodied sock being stowed away for use as possible evidence, she could've believed she'd imagined that whole thing. Bud had eaten the muffins. The log had simply fallen. And the island was a little too perfect a setting. Which was the only reason she even had time to ponder her feelings for the man she'd been assigned to protect.

He sighed. "Picnics just aren't my thing. Willow used to take Meggie on them all the time. In the backyard, to any park with swings or ducks." He tapped his fork against the edge of his plate.

"You were invited?"

"Well, yeah. Sure, I went, too. It's just…I don't know. Hard being on a picnic with anyone but them."

"You seemed fine the other day."

"I was. But why tempt fate by doing it again?"

"Sure… Can I ask you a question?" Gillian blurted.

"Go for it." He eased back in his chair.

"Do you find me attractive?"

Ramrod straight again, he said, "What the hell kind of question is that?"

She raised her chin. "Don't read anything into it. I'd just like a man's perspective. When we get off of this rock, I'm thinking about throwing myself back into the dating pool and—"

Leaning across the table, he reached for her hand. "You're *very* pretty—and smart. Any guy would be lucky to have you."

"Really?"

"What're you going for here, because I know you're not dumb enough to think for one second you're not a good-looking woman."

Woman. Funny, but in her mind, she still saw herself as a girl. Not big enough to play her brothers' games. Certainly not mature enough to be part of a relationship. It was for the best that she and Kent had gone separate ways. She wasn't ready for more. "Did you like being married?"

"Mmm." He flashed her a weak smile. "Another off-the-wall question."

"You know what I mean. The day-to-day stuff. Did it ever get boring? I mean, did you ever just wake up thinking, man, this just isn't working out? I've gotta have my own space?"

He took a second to think about it, then said, "Nope. Don't get me wrong, me and Willow had our share of fights about the usual things. Her spending too much on clothes. Me spending too much time at work. But over-all, she was my world. Guess that's why I'm having such a hard time being in a world without her. Just doesn't fit."

"Sorry."

He shrugged before grabbing both of their plates, then heading for the sink. "If you're not currently even dating anyone, what do you care about marriage?"

"I don't."

He filled a big pot with water, then turned on the stove to heat it.

"I was just curious, that's all. About what it's like—being married. Nothing personal." Like wondering if she were to ever meet a guy like him outside of a work situation, if things might be this good. This easy. Sure, she'd enjoyed her time with Kent, but she'd never once experienced this magnetic hum of perfection.

"Come on, Bud." She pushed back her chair. "Let's go outside so I can set the alarms before conking out."

The dog just sat on his pillow looking at her.

"Tired?" Joe asked from the sink.

She nodded before taking her jacket from the peg beside the door.

Bud slowly made his way, toenails clicking, after her.

"Let me take him," Joe said. "The fog's cleared since we went fishing. Bet your fellow good guys are doing a swell job patrolling my shores."

"Right. They're doing their job, meaning I should do mine—not you."

"You PMSing?"

Casting him the mother of all glares, she said, "You didn't just say that."

He dried his hands on a dish towel before tucking his hands in his jeans pockets, casually strolling her way. A smile played about the corners of his full, sensual mouth, but there was nothing happy in his eyes. They read intensity. Heat. "What are you going to do if I did?"

He stood so close, she could've reached out and grabbed a fistful of his smooth cotton T-shirt. She could have slipped her other hand over the dimple at the back of his neck, pulling him into a kiss that would rock both their worlds.

She could've done all that, but being a professional, she settled for just licking her lips.

"Christ, what're you doing to me?" he said, close enough that his warm breath did the kissing for him.

Grabbing the open sides of her jacket, he eliminated the space between them, closing his eyes before resting his forehead against hers.

Afraid her legs might buckle beneath her, she said, "I—I'm not on my period."

"I know."

How?

"Guys aren't dumb. Especially not married guys."

"But you're not married anymore."

"I still think like I'm married."

Then why are you holding me?

He skimmed his broad hands, his long strong fingers, up the sides of her face and into her hair, freeing it of its scrunchie. He held her hair, shifting to bring some to his nose. "I love the smell of this stuff. Any guy would."

I'm terrified that I don't want any guy. *Just you.*

"Let me take care of Bud."

From somewhere, she found the strength to shake her head. With narrowed eyes, she made out the shape of his mouth. Her lips tingled from craving him. Not just his touch, but his taste. "You shouldn't go outside."

"I'm the man. Dog walking is my duty."

"Protecting you is *my* duty." Her heart hammered, as

did his. She felt it pounding against her. "I can't do this," she softly said.

"Me, neither."

Bud whined. Scratched at the door.

"So what do you want to do?" Joe asked, easing his broad hands down her back, putting her in far more danger than she'd ever been in from a mere gun-toting thug. That was just her work. This, standing in the circle of Joe's all-too-capable arms, was the real deal.

What did she want to do?

Forget Tsun-Chung's trial even existed. Forget her father and brothers and career, and focus solely on Joe. His taste, touch. His taking her roughly, right there on the floor in a crushing union that made her forget everything she thought she was and ever wanted to be.

She wanted him.

Only him.

But it was wrong, and so she stepped away, then called out to the dog.

Her hand on the doorknob, she was pulling the door shut when Joe said, "Gillian?"

"Uh-huh?"

"Your, um, eyes look red. Like your allergies are bugging you. Want me to put more drops in them when you get back?"

"Yes, please," she murmured, drawing the door closed, trying to ignore the contentment his simple, sweet caring sent shimmering through her body.

Chapter Eleven

"Joe, nothing happened last night." The next morning, Gillian begrudgingly followed Joe along a trail so heavily wooded, it almost felt as if they were marching through a cave. And make no mistake, they were marching. Joe seemed driven by an invisible wolf pack nipping at his heels. If she had her way, they wouldn't have left the house. Her unease was back, along with a queasy, prickly sensation that something far more than Joe's grumpy mood wasn't right. "We didn't even kiss, if that's what has you so upset."

"I'm not upset," he said, not even remotely out of breath. "You're right. Nothing happened." He'd outpaced her by a good five yards.

She jogged to catch up. "She died two years ago, Joe. The statute of limitations for cheating on your dead wife is long past."

"Dammit," he barked, stopping so abruptly on the trail they almost collided. "Would you mind your own business and just stay out of it?"

"I find you hot, all right?" She looked away. "There.

I said it. It's unprofessional as all get-out, but there it is. Out there on the table. If you want to be mad at someone for breaking your wedding vows, it's me, okay? I started whatever *didn't* happen between us."

"The hell you did," he growled from between clenched teeth.

"Great." Hands on her hips, she said, "Now that we're both to blame, what do you want to do about it?"

He drank her in a tick longer than eternity, then pulled her hard against him, grinding his lips to hers, moaning from somewhere deep in his throat. By unspoken mutual consent, their lips parted, deepening wild sensations with bold strokes of their tongues.

With fingers shaky and uncertain, and a heart hammering with both fear and exhilaration, Gillian slid her hands under Joe's T-shirt. Up his smooth back.

He did the same to her, only took a different course over her right breast, never breaching the sanctity of her silky bra no matter how much her nipple swelled and ached in invitation.

All around them, the dark forest breathed, bearing silent witness as each trespass unfolded.

And yet the kiss went on and on, until Gillian was sinking to her knees, taking Joe along with her. "Oh, God," she said in a hoarse whisper. "I'm so sorry."

"Me, too," he said, kissing her deeper still. His arousal pulsed against her. "This changes everything."

She nodded. Shook her head. "It's my job to protect you. How can I do that when I'm seducing you?"

"No," he said against her forehead. "It's the other way around."

"Do you think it's possible no one's at fault? You know, just that it's been a long time since… Well, you know, for both of us, and that this is just a chemistry kind of thing?"

Nodding against her, he said, "Yeah. Chemistry." In a move that somehow felt more intimate than their kiss, Joe took her hands, easing his fingers between hers. "Wanna resume that walk?"

"We weren't walking. We were marching."

"Sorry." With the faintest grin, he said, "I have issues. Walking—marching—helps."

"H—how about strolling?"

"We could do that."

"Any sign of Bud?" Gillian glanced over her shoulder to see the dog stretched out on a pillow of pine needles with his head resting on his front paws. He looked at them sleepily.

"Guess we had an audience, huh?" Joe closed his eyes and groaned. "Good grief, what a mess." Looking back at her, squeezing her hands, he added, "But it doesn't have to be. From here on out, if you promise to look a little less appealing, I promise to keep my hands to myself."

"Oh, so now that kiss was all my fault?"

He winked. "Sure beats keeping all the blame for myself."

He was no expert, but to Joe, the glade they napped in felt straight out of Disney.

Spongy green moss, glassy spring-fed pond. Soaring pines and a sprinkling of early spring grasses and flowers. Sun rays punched through the pine bough roof, heating the air, supercharging rich scents of soil and water and Gillian's hair.

While Bud napped in the sun, Joe kissed the top of Gillian's head, where she lay using the crook of his shoulder for a pillow. She softly snored. Were her allergies bothering her again? Was she hungry? He should've insist she bring more to eat.

Geez, listen to him.

He sounded like her father, not her…what? What had he become to her? What did he want to be?

They were friends. That was it. It was her job to protect him. Friends were all they could ever be.

Kissing friends?

Sighing, he sliced his fingers through his hair before settling beside her, indulging in a nap himself.

GILLIAN'S HEART THUNDERED. Joe. Tsun-Chung held him in a headlock, his left arm wrapped so tight around Joe's throat that his face was turning red.

"Kindly put down your gun or I'll kill him." The look in the man's eyes said he'd kill both of them—no matter what Gillian did with her piece. "Need me to say please?" He smiled. "All right, then, please put down your gun or I'll place my own weapon in his mouth and shoot off his blabbering tongue."

"Get out of here," Joe said to her, past blueing lips. "Save yourself."

"No," she said with a violent shake of her head. "It's my job to protect you. I won't—"

"Gillian? You all right?"

She woke with a start.

Joe? She had to save him.

Only there he was, resting on his elbow, staring down at her as if he was concerned. Pulse still racing, drenched in sweat, Gillian followed her first instinct, which was to reach up and touch his dear face.

She couldn't be sure when it'd happened, maybe the first time she'd seen his sad eyes in the photos in his files, but he *had* become dear to her. She'd never push him for more than friendship. By his own admission, he wasn't capable of more. She was on assignment, forbidden to give more.

So what was she doing, lying here in a fairy tale glade, napping in his arms, when for all she knew, her nightmare could at any time turn real?

"If it's not too personal," Joe asked, fingering strands of her hair, "what were you dreaming about? Didn't sound pleasant."

"Nothing." She shook her head. Swallowed hard before flashing a smile. "Just one of those college dreams where it's exam day, only I've never been to class."

"Guilty conscience, huh?" He winked.

"About not keeping a better eye on you?"

"No. Hell, no. Where could I be that's safer than right here? I was talking about college. You know, like were you one of those who skipped a lot of classes?"

She reached into her backpack for bottled water.

Even lukewarm, it felt good going down, but unfortunately didn't do a thing to calm her nerves.

Behind them, a good twenty feet to their left, a twig snapped.

She jerked her head that direction, only to see a rabbit bolt, soon followed by a slow-moving Bud.

Joe was right. She needed to relax.

It had just been a dream.

"Well?" he asked, reaching for the bottle and taking a swig. To see him drinking after her, curving his lips around the same plastic where hers had just touched, implied an intimacy her heart couldn't bear. "Did you skip a lot?"

"Nah," she said, struggling to act as if she wasn't deeply affected by the man's every move, touch and expression. "Going back to my whole beef with my dad and brothers, I always felt like I had to do better than them in all of my courses."

"Did you?"

"Heck, yeah. Graduated second in my college class. First at the training academy in Glynco."

"Way to go." He whistled. "My grades sucked. I was always more of a doer than a thinker. Couldn't stand having my head in a book on business when I could be out there doing the real thing."

"That's cool. And look where you are in the world versus me—barely able to afford my own apartment, and here you own an island."

He shrugged. "Money isn't everything. What you do, Gillian—protecting people—it's important."

"Thank you." Coming from him, oddly, the compliment felt better than it might've from someone else.

Laughing, shaking his head, he said, "Can't believe with these kinds of academic credentials behind you that

I'm your first field case. You could be a real life Charlie's Angel." He winked.

She made a face.

"HELLO, SUNSHINE," Wesson said with a slow grin. "Have a nice nap?"

For a second there, right after Logue first woke, she'd stared right at him. Good thing she was so pathetic she didn't know the difference between a tree and a man. Good thing he'd set out that drugged piece of meat for that stupid dog. Dumb mutt was moving slow, and likely, his senses were all messed up.

Watching Logue like this, slowly building appetites he couldn't wait to fulfill, the only way he kept sane was by thinking of good times yet to come. Like planning an intricate dinner party, he wanted everything about her death to be just right. The pain—lots. The mess—even more. He hated women. He hated her above all the others.

They'd dated once.

Bitch didn't even remember.

He'd remind her.

Nice and slow, with the same kind of steak knife she'd used to plow through their hundred-dollar meal. And while she was still enjoying that little trip down memory lane, how she'd oh-so-politely pushed him away when he'd tried kissing her good-night, he'd take good care of her new boyfriend. Real good care.

Wesson laughed—but not too loud. Not loudly enough to wake the dead. For that's what Logue and Morgan were.

AFTER DINNER, Joe stoked the fire while Gillian read a spy novel she'd found stashed among the classics on his

shelves. He never brought anything with him to the island but his dog and a few clothes. Before Gil's arrival,
he hadn't paid much attention to the items left behind
by the island's previous owners, but she'd unearthed everything from tablecloths to games to extra blankets.

She sat in his roomy armchair, bare feet tucked beside her. She'd changed from jeans and a navy T-shirt
into gray sweats. Her ponytail was messier than usual,
and every so often she'd twirl escaped strands of hair.

With the fire crackling, Bud curled on his hearth bed
and the light of two oil lamps asking the shadows to
dance, it was hard to fathom why Gillian felt she had to
protect him.

She curled her fingers over her bare toes.

"Cold feet?" he asked.

She glanced up and smiled. "A little, but it's no big
deal."

Lost again in her book, she didn't notice him slipping
to his dresser for a pair of thick, white socks.

Back again, he said, "Stick out your feet."

"What?" Setting her book on her lap, she looked up
at him and scrunched her nose.

He held up her prize.

She stuck out her feet, wriggled red-tipped toes.
"How sweet. Thanks."

Down on one knee in front of her, he shrugged, trying to pretend he wasn't fascinated by the cute foot, slim
ankle and gently curved calf she'd rested on his thigh.
Her toes were icy to the touch, reminding him why he
was putting himself through the torture of skimming his
hands along her smooth legs—because she was cold.
Not because he was all of a sudden uncomfortably hot.

Chapter Twelve

"Can't sleep?" Joe asked, rubbing his eyes in the intrusive bathroom light.

Gillian sat hunched over the tub, scrubbing grout with a ratty toothbrush. The harsh scent of Comet did even more to bring him wide-awake.

"Isn't it pretty obvious?"

He scratched his head. "All right, then, maybe the better question is how come?"

"When I'm nervous, I clean."

"Why?" He sat on the closed toilet lid.

"You mean why do I clean instead of biting my nails or eating?"

"Why are you nervous?"

She scrubbed harder. "As a field marshal, I'm a joke. This afternoon I actually fell sleep in your arms. Then tonight, I'm letting you put on my socks. Not cool. My dad and brothers were right. I should've just settled down. Gotten married and popped out a few babies—only gee, I couldn't even hold on to the only man I ever even considered marrying."

What about me? Would you marry me, Gil?

The thought hit hard and fast, shocking Joe to his core. It was the late hour and the cleanser's fumes making him irrational. Not the sight of Gillian's crazy-messy hair or ragged blue sweats she'd cut into shorts. Shorts baring far too much of her tanned legs. Shorts with a hole on her left hip, through which a patch of pale skin peeked through. Just looking at that skin, wondering about its feel and taste, quickened his pulse.

These kinds of thoughts were wrong. Gillian was here to do a job. He was for all practical purposes married.

So why was he taking the toothbrush from her, laying it on the side of the tub, then easing his hands under her elbows, urging her to her feet?

When she stood facing him with the top of her head reaching his chin, he took her left hand, leading her into the dark breakfast nook.

He swished open the drapes he kept closed at night more for insulation than privacy.

Beyond the picture window, far out on the restless sea, moonlight glinted off the windshield of a cabin cruiser. "Look," he said, pulling her closer, pointing toward her co-workers.

"It's supposed to make me feel better that because I'm a total screwup, my boss thoughtfully provided backup?"

"Knock it off, Gillian." Joe sighed. "What you do is too dangerous to handle alone. Like it or not, you're part of a team. Truth is, your boss was right in sending you. Those guys out there probably wouldn't have had a chance at bringing me in for the trial. I'd have bolted.

Fast. But you…" He laughed, scratched the new crop of stubble on his jaw. "You are a true force to contend with."

"What's that mean?"

"What do you think?" At the gas-powered fridge, he took out leftovers of the potato casserole she had made for dinner. From the rack hanging above the stove, he grabbed a small, copper-bottomed pan, set it on a front burner, then dumped the cheesy mixture in before turning on the stove. "I never even had a chance at holding on to my old way of life. Sharing this place with you— it's changed…"

Everything.

To a degree he was terrified to explore.

"Great," she said, taking a bag of pizza-flavored Goldfish from the cabinet beside the sink. Days earlier, she'd merged her food with his. Her shampoo and toothpaste and perfumed soap. Joe's stomach tightened just thinking of the way the soft, pretty scent emanated from her after she'd worked up a good sweat. "So I've changed you, even though all I'm supposed to be doing is protecting you. God." She brushed stray hair back from her forehead. "I never should've taken down my tent. I should've stayed in there. Much safer—for both of us."

He wanted to argue the point, but how could he when he agreed?

She stepped past him to the stove, pulled out a serving spoon from the pottery crock where she'd stowed all of his big utensils. "Your snack's burning," she said, reaching to stir the hissing, crackling cheese and canned milk.

"Let me do that," he said. "You've still got Comet on your hands."

With a sad laugh, she looked down. "Great. I'm no good at man jobs or woman jobs. I can't even remember to wash my hands before cooking."

"You weren't cooking. I was. And for the record, before you started preparing meals around here, never once did I have the urge for a late-night snack. Bud got all the leftovers. So see? If you're implying cooking is a woman's job, you're not just good at it, but great."

She stood at the sink, staring at the faucet, her small hands gripping the counter's edge.

He wanted so badly to hug her. So why had his arms turned to lead?

He hadn't just kissed her on more than one occasion, but devoured her, so why now, when she so clearly needed some kind of warmth, did he just stand there like a goon, not sure what to say or do?

The only thing he did know for sure was that he was no good for her. She needed a man who still had feelings and sensitivity and—screw that.

After taking the pan off the stove, then turning off the burner, he yanked her hard by her upper arm over to the bed.

"What the—"

"Take it from an expert on self-pity, Gil, it's time for you—hell, both of us—to start seeing our glasses as half-full. As you love reminding me, I've got a daughter out there needing a dad."

"Right. And what do I have after botching your case? Nothing."

"Bull." He sat her down on the edge of the bed, then reached to the nightstand for the silver star glinting in pale moonlight. He took her clenched hand, forced her fingers open and pressed the star into her palm. "The day you first got here, you flashed me this badge with a look so fierce I knew I'd met my match. Yeah, I can be stubborn, but you, woman, are a friggin' full-force gale. Remember how you trailed after me? Never giving me a moment's peace until you finally wore me down to the point where I no longer wanted peace?" *All I wanted was you. The sound of your voice. Your laugh.* He softened his tone. "I'm your first field case, Gil. Cut yourself some slack."

"Oh, that's rich." Closing her fingers around her badge, she half sniffled, half laughed. "Coming from a guy who's spent the past two years running from something that wasn't even his fault."

"Don't you dare bring Willow's death into this. If I'd just kept my mouth shut, none of this would've ever happened. I never should've gone to the cops in the first place. I should've—"

"Let hundreds, maybe thousands more people be hurt by this guy's ever-growing web? Yes, it was horrible that Willow died, but how is that any more your fault than it's my fault—" She put her free hand over her mouth.

"My point exactly." Despite his own heavy emotional losses, Joe couldn't help cracking a smile. "It's not your fault that nothing remotely exciting in the way of gunplay has happened since you got here? That bad guys aren't hiding behind every rock? Rappelling down every cliff?"

"Stop." She smacked his chest.

He took her hand in his, giving it the squeeze he wanted to give her whole body.

"This is serious to me, Joe. It's my job to protect you. Yet…" Gillian gazed up into his face. Into the hard planes softened by shadows. What had she been on the verge of admitting? All she wanted to do was kiss him, then kiss him again? That more than wanting to protect him, she wanted him to protect her? And love her and make sure her allergy drops actually went into her eyes, before reading to her while she fell asleep? And to cover her cold toes with his warm socks and to call her during endless days at work spent filing and filling out paperwork?

"We should get some sleep." She put her silver star back on the nightstand, then covered her face with her hands. "Tomorrow I need to brief you a little more on what to expect at the trial."

"I know what to expect," he said, his hands on her shoulder. "In case you've forgotten, I've kind of been through it before."

"Yes, but—"

"Lie down."

"What?" She gasped when he scooped her up, only to set her sideways on the bed.

"For once in your life, Gil, loosen up. Let someone else take care of you. Who knows? You might end up liking it." He lay down beside her, tugging her close.

"I can't *like* it, Joe." She wriggled, attempting to escape. "In case you've forgotten, it's not only against my work rules, but every rule I've established for myself since, like, the fourth grade. I'm a strong, capable woman. I don't need some guy around to—"

"Kiss?" Rolling atop her, he cradled her cheek with

his hand, pressing his lips to hers in such a way that it wasn't smothering or controlling, just thrilling and exhilarating, like all things forbidden tend to be. Only just when it really started getting good, just when her belly tingled and nipples hardened and ached, he stopped, rolling off her to once again settle behind her, his hand curved around her stomach, his nose tucked in her hair. "You smell good," he said. "Like normalcy. I don't know about you, but I could use a big dose of that."

Easing her hand over his, she nodded, closed her eyes and succumbed to sleep.

SOMETIME IN THE MIDDLE of the night, Gillian bolted upright. "Bud?"

The dog growled.

It wasn't his playful bark and growl-at-tidal-pool-crabs routine, but a serious, throaty, get-the-hell-out-of-my-cabin growl.

While Joe slept soundly beside her, she slipped her legs out from under the sheet and thick quilts.

The fire had gone out, and the room's only light was a faint stream of moonlight spilling through the part in the breakfast nook curtains.

Bud growled again, and she tiptoed by memory to the pine wardrobe where she'd stashed her gun. When the door creaked open, she spilled a hundred silent curses.

Gun in hand, she cursed again, wishing she hadn't considered night-vision goggles as supply overkill.

The cabin's air was cold.

Thin.

Deathly quiet.

Then Bud growled yet again, his nails click-clacking on the back hall's hardwood floor.

Gillian's throat tightened. Nostrils flared. Stomach clenched. Pulse hammered in her ears.

Had she only imagined the faint click of the back door opening, the faintest lowering of temperature, change in smell?

"I've got a gun," she said to the darkness. "I'm not afraid to use it."

Another click?

The door closing?

Never had she wished more for a nice, convenient electric light. Joe kept a flashlight in the drawer to the right of the stove, so she crept that way, finding it more by feel than sight.

With the light in one hand, her piece in the other, she cocked the trigger, then flicked on the light and jumped.

Bud stared up at her and whined.

Flashlight hand to her chest, she breathed for the first time in the past two minutes.

A quick scan of the open living-sleeping-kitchen area showed it was empty. With her back to the wall adjacent to the hall, she held her arms out straight in front of her, crossing them at the wrists, light on top, weapon on the bottom.

Heart pounding, she spun fast, aiming her light and gun down the hall, toward the back door.

The closed and locked back door.

She followed the same procedure for checking out the bathroom, but that room was clean, too.

The dog looked up at her and cocked his head. "Was

someone in here?" she whispered. "Tell me, Bud, did I just dream this whole thing? You growling? The click of the opening and closing door?"

The dog infuriatingly kept his secrets, as did the tomb-quiet cabin.

WESSON BROUGHT LOGUE'S dirty T-shirt to his nose and breathed deeply. Mmm. Nice. He might hate women, but not their smell. Those fragrant, man-teasing potions they rubbed all over their soft bellies and breasts, calves and inner thighs.

Perched on his favorite outcropping of rocks high above the cabin, Wesson smiled, fingering the shirt's soft, navy cotton.

That'd been close, he thought with a giggle.

For a minute there, he'd thought he just might have to gut that meddling dog. Not that he couldn't have handled it. He was more of a cat man, himself. Still, now that he had a firm plan, he hated deviating from it.

Amateurs killed just to kill. Or because they'd been caught off guard and had to. Wesson, on the other hand, had always fancied himself to be the consummate professional.

And so he was now quite happy to allow Kavorski his extra days. Because what the old fart didn't know was that he'd soon be dying, too.

For suddenly just two deaths weren't enough—oh, but then he'd already done his partner, poor Finch. How could he have forgotten that little bit of fun? But every dinner party needed an appetizer, and the handsome young stud had gallantly filled that role, his dying words full of sappy-ass love for his wife. Next came the main course. And then Kavorski would be a satisfying, pallet-cleansing dessert. A sherbet, or sorbet if you will.

Not too filling or rich, but just right.

The perfect end to the perfect little killing spree.

"DAMN, GIRL. Those are some white-hot reflexes you got there."

Gillian had caught Joe as he fell down the front porch steps. "You okay?" she asked, trying not to notice how close they stood, trying not to remember how much closer they'd been all night—at least until… No. She wasn't going to think about what she'd only *thought* had happened. The dark was naturally an unnerving place. Bud had been growling at a mouse.

"I am now," Joe said. "If you hadn't been here, that might've been a nasty fall."

"Yeah, well…" She shrugged, shading her eyes from the bright morning sun. "We'd better get going. Looks like Bud's got a head start." The dog had already crossed the flower-strewn meadow beside the cabin and was loping into the forest, baying the whole way.

Releasing Joe, Gillian headed after Bud.

Until leaving the island for the trial, she figured it'd be best if they engaged in physical activities other than kissing, hugging or sharing Joe's bed. Which was why, after she'd prepared them both a quick breakfast of oatmeal and canned pears, they were now headed across the island to explore an abandoned cabin Joe had told her about two nights earlier at dinner.

"Slow down," he said. "Want me to get a hernia?"

Hands on her hips, she scanned the area before turning and shooting him a bright smile. "Point of fact. I'm pretty sure you can't get a hernia by hiking."

"I might if I had to lift a log off the trail."

"You're reaching."

He winked.

They'd been on the trail a whole five minutes when Joe nearly poked his eye out with a low-hanging limb. Luckily, Gillian caught him before he'd run right into it.

"Beautiful maiden saves my butt again. Thanks."

"You're welcome. Only it was your eye."

"Eye, butt. Close enough."

They made it a whole fifteen minutes farther down the trail before Joe met his next catastrophe—stepping too close to the edge of a steep drop-off. Yanking him back to safe ground as a flurry of pebbles skipped down the cliff, Gillian said, "What's the matter with you? I've never seen you so careless. If I didn't know better, I'd swear you were…" She narrowed her eyes. "Are you purposely trying to hurt yourself?"

"Why would I do that?"

"To get out of testifying."

"But I want to testify."

"So why are you dead set on breaking a limb?"

"I'm not."

"Did you know your left eyebrow twitches when you lie?"

"And you know this how?"

"The other night when I made garbage casserole out of stewed tomatoes, macaroni and cheese, and added a little leftover spaghetti?"

"Yeah?" He looked queasy just thinking about it.

"Remember when I asked if you liked it, and you just raved and raved about how good it was?"

"Sure. It was, um, great." He turned, but not fast enough for her to miss his poor little eyebrow twitching away.

"Which must be why you fed it to Bud when I got up for a refill on iced tea?"

"You caught that?"

Hands on her hips, she rolled her eyes. "Give me some credit."

"Okay, so I'm busted on one count of feeding Bud your dinner, but why would I be lying right now?"

"There," she said, putting her finger over the telltale spot. Though instinct told her to snatch her finger back the instant it began tingling from Joe's heat, she kept it there, on his eyebrow, smoothing it down his temple, cheek and jaw. "You're doing it again. What you up to, Joe?"

Sighing, he grabbed for her finger, kissing it before linking his hand with hers. "It was stupid." He looked down. "Especially that last stunt. But what the hell…" He shrugged. "It worked. At least until my stupid eyebrow gave me away. Willow used to say the same thing. About that twitching."

"All of those close calls? Then they were on purpose?"

"Sort of."

"What do you mean, *sort of?* Did you or did you not do all that stuff on purpose? And if so, why?"

Though her hands were still on her hips, Joe slid his arms around her, tugging her against him. "Would you believe I did all that for you?"

"But why?"

"Because if only for a few minutes, it brought back your smile." He traced her lips. "You seemed so sad last night about not needing to protect me, I figured what the hell? I'd give you a little more to do."

She grabbed his finger, which was still paused on her lower lip, and bit it.

"Ouch. What was that for?"

"Because I'm mad at you—furious. Geez, Joe, what you did was incredibly sweet, but at the same time, condescending. It's exactly the kind of stunt my dad or brothers would pull."

"And why do you think they do those kinds of things? Did it ever occur to you that they might want to see you happy? Not out of some need to control you, but simply because they love you?"

"Do you love me, Joe?" The question was out before she'd realized the implications of asking.

Once she had, though, she took off at a dead run. Not caring about the brambles tearing at her bare arms or jeans. Not caring that Bud thought she was playing a game, and chased after her. She especially didn't care that Joe wasn't following.

Oh no, because if she had, then that might imply another question. One infinitely more personal and borderline insane, considering how long Joe and she had been acquainted. One that she would never voice aloud, and wished she couldn't even think.

Do I love you, Joe? Is that why what you just did hurts?

Out of breath, she stopped. Bud nudged his cold, wet nose into her palm.

She connected with his deep brown eyes. "Wanna know something even worse than that question?" she whispered.

The dog continued staring.

"I think I fell for Joe the first time I saw the haunted look on his face at the last trial."

Bud licked her.

"That your way of saying sorry that I—meaning me—did something so dumb?" She scratched the dog behind his big, lovable ears. "I'm sorry, too, sweetie."

"SORRY, SIR," the kid said, binoculars held so close to his eyes they looked like a damn alien growth. "Can't see either of them this morning."

"You're not certain Mr. Morgan is in the cabin?" Kavorski asked.

"No, sir. Logue took the dog out early this morning. Then Mr. Morgan followed. But I can't be a hundred percent sure either of them has returned."

"Keep looking." Kavorski bit into the bologna and American cheese sandwich he'd made for lunch.

Geesh, he hated this food. Been eating it at least once a day for the past twenty years. Why? He snorted. Sure as hell not because it tasted good. More likely because it was cheap and filling. His doc said he needed to cut down his salt. Said that played a big part in his medical problems.

When this was over, following doctors' orders would be a whole lot easier. After a light morning workout with a Swedish, stacked personal trainer named Inga, he'd dine on lobster and Hooter's hot wings. Buckets and buckets of the damn things. Surely there wasn't much salt in those, was there?

The plan to off Logue and the canary was so easy, sometimes Kavorski felt guilty actually taking so much cash to see it through. But generally the guilt didn't last. Then he was back to planning how good life would be once the two lovebirds were gone.

Chapter Thirteen

"You're awfully quiet," Joe said, while Gillian stared at her bowl of canned chili.

The supper had been uninspired. Kind of like the rest of that day.

He should've gone after her, but when she'd asked that question—the one about love—he'd thought his heart might stop. But then it'd started up again, hammering so hard he'd worried he was having some kind of attack.

Yeah, he knew full well the only reason he was attracted to Gillian had way more to do with chemistry than anything deeper—like the *L* word—so why was he still so uneasy? Because it was going to be a nightmare second only to losing Willow and Meggie when the trial ended and it was time for Gillian and him to say goodbye?

"What's there to talk about?" she said, swirling the tasteless, heartburn-inducing red glop.

"For starters, why'd you run off today? Killer squirrels and bunnies might've ravaged me while you were on a leisurely jog."

She treated him to a cold glare. "Thanks for taking my job so seriously."

"Done playing with that?" he asked, eyeing her bowl.

She shoved it his way. He used her spoon to eat the rest.

"Eeuw." Nose scrunched, she said, "How can you stand eating that stuff?"

He shrugged. "Not much choice, seeing how nobody volunteered to make me anything else."

"Oh, like it's part of my job description to cook for you?"

Smirking, he said, "You were the one who first made me that French toast. If you'd never shown me what a great cook you are, then I now wouldn't be craving more of your tasty concoctions—except for that garbage can stuff." He made a face.

"Let me get this straight. It's my fault you're a chauvinist?"

"That hurts." He clutched his chest. "More than chili heartburn."

"If the shoe fits…" she said with a sweet smile.

"What can I do to redeem myself?"

"Hmm…" Finger to her lips, she said, "Unless you have a deep-pan pizza with Canadian bacon, black olives and pineapple, I'm afraid you're pretty much out of luck."

"Okay, yeah, pizza's out, but what about…" He left the table to rummage in a cabinet high above the stove. Seeing how Gillian couldn't begin to reach it, she'd never even tried. "This." He returned to the table brandishing a box of chocolate chip cookie mix.

"Where'd you get that?" She snatched the box.

"Carl—you know, the guy who stocks the cabin? His wife slipped it into my regular shipment when I was here around Christmas."

"Why haven't you eaten it?"

The truth? Joe hadn't felt worthy. Hadn't wanted to indulge himself in one of life's little pleasures. He felt responsible for Willow's death. For leaving Meggie without a mother or father. For putting her in continued danger just because of what he knew.

Yes, he paid damn well to insure his daughter was under round-the-clock protection, but who was to say, as Gillian had so thoughtfully pointed out, that Tsun-Chung wouldn't one day try kidnapping her? Using her as a bargaining chip to get to her dad? What Gil didn't know was that Joe had already played that scenario in his head. If it came down to it, he'd give his life for his daughter's in a heartbeat.

"Joe?" Gillian shook the box. "These look delicious. Why haven't you scarfed them down months ago?"

"No need."

"This is about you shouldering blame, isn't it?"

"What if it is?"

She rubbed her forehead. "You've gotta work past this."

"Oh, like you've gotten past what it was like living under the watchful eyes of your dad and brothers?"

"That's different."

"How?"

"Because my issues with them aren't unhealthy."

His once concerned features turned to stone. "I'm sick of talking about this. I'm out of here."

"The hell you are. We were talking about *you*. My

father and brothers are all big boys. What about your little girl, Joe? My family doesn't miss me in the least, but Meghan needs you."

"Unlike you? Who'll never need anyone?"

Joe couldn't have hurt her more if he'd socked her in her gut. Whoever had coined that old adage *the truth hurts* had been a little too smart. Gillian squeezed the cookie box so hard the plastic bag inside popped. Fine white powder puffed from the top.

Joe shot her one last indescribably cold look before walking out the door.

Bud glanced up from his cushion beside the fire, then fell back to sleep with his head on his paws.

Had Gillian been a true marshal, instead of the wannabe her brothers and father knew she was, she would've chased after Joe.

No matter how ticked she was at him, she shouldn't have let him leave the cabin for even a second without her. But no, here she sat, feeling sorry for herself. Fighting back stupid, irrational tears over how she'd never be good enough to compete in a man's world.

She was trying to decide between whether to bake and then eat the entire box of cookies, or just go to bed, when it dawned on her that if she went with either of those choices, she would have become exactly what her family wanted. A nice, safe, stay-at-home wife. Baking cookies. Waiting for her man to come home. Only she'd always been better at homemade cheesecake than cookies, and Joe wasn't her man, but her assignment. And by God, no matter how much he ticked her off, she wasn't about to let him get hurt on her watch.

"WE'RE SOME PAIR, HUH?" Gillian found Joe standing at the edge of the cliff where they'd shared their first civil conversation what seemed liked months earlier, but had actually only been a little over a week.

"You *do* have issues," he said above the roar of the wind, staring out at a churning black sea. "I'm not the only one."

"I know." She hunched deeper into her jacket, noticing that Bud had followed her and now stood sentry by her leg. "I'm, ah, sorry for implying you're solo in the issues department." She stood beside Joe, and he slipped his arm about her shoulders, flooding her heart and body with forbidden warmth. She shouldn't be standing here with him like this. Exposed. Physically, emotionally, in every way she could. Granted, it was dark, but not dark enough to avoid night-vision goggles or high-powered rifle scopes or worse—succumbing to his spell.

"You really think Meghan would want to see me?"

Swallowing hard past the instant knot in her throat, Gillian nodded. "I—I think she'd be thrilled to see you."

"If I agree to go back to being a full-time dad, would you have it out with the men in your life? You know, ask them to stop meddling? Treat you like a professional instead of a child?"

She sighed. "Am I a professional? I came out here to do a job, but after the way I've acted with you…"

Where they stood at the edge of a two-hundred-foot-high cliff, surf violently crashing below, they were literally one step away from death. Yet, since moving in with Joe, Gillian had never felt more alive. At the start of this mission, she'd wanted nothing more than professional glory. Now she wanted that and more.

To wake every day to the sound of Joe's even breathing beside her. To know the feel of his hands caressing her naked body. Beyond that, in the innermost reaches of her heart, she imagined the joy of carrying his son or daughter inside her. The pride of watching Meghan ace a ballet recital.

"What're you thinking?" Joe asked, leaning close enough that they felt connected.

"Believe me," she said with a tight laugh, "you don't want to know."

"Try me."

After a deep breath, she gave him the abridged version. "It was pretty lame, actually. You know, just wondering how things might be between us if we'd met under different circumstances. Like before you'd ever even met Willow or before I'd adopted my whole, I-am-woman, hear-me-roar routine."

"How's any of that lame?"

"Because I'm here to do my job, and you're here to mourn your wife. I mean, where could the two of us possibly go?"

"Aw…ISN'T THAT SWEET?" Wesson said in regards to Logue's latest sappy remark to Morgan.

Wesson had wired the whole place for sound days ago. Put a microtransmitter on the mutt's collar. Made it handier for those on-the-go occasions when the lovebirds took off on their epic hikes.

Exercise had never been Wesson's thing. He didn't care for sweat. Made him itch.

From his seat at the cabin's kitchen table, he cranked up the volume on his receiver.

Hearing the two of them go at it almost made up for the island's lack of cable TV.

But he needed snacks. Having already finished off the chili in both their bowls, he eyed the box of cookie mix and smiled.

Could he be so brazen as to fix the couple a lovely surprise treat?

Why not?

Everyone deserved a little fun before dying.

"SMELLS GOOD IN HERE," Gillian said upon their return. She slipped off her jacket, tossed it over the back of the sofa, then froze.

"What's that?" Joe asked, pointing at the perfect pyramid of chocolate chip cookies on the table. "I'm gone," he said a second later, already at the door.

"Wait," Gillian said. "There has to be an explanation."

"There's no time for this," Joe said. "You coming?"

"Wait!" From under the kitchen cabinet, Gillian fished out her radio. "Kavorski? Brimmer? Finch? Wesson? Dammit, one of you answer me!"

"Wesson. What's up, Gillie?"

"You been up here?" she said into the mic, trying to hide the trembling of her hands.

"Huh? You mean to the cabin?"

"Yes, dammit."

"Thirty seconds till I'm a ghost," Joe said.

"I take it you found my present?"

"You left the cookies?" Gillian asked, relief sagging her shoulders.

"Well, actually, it was Finch's idea." He laughed. "Poor kid, he's been sick as shit. Missing his wife. Apparently the sea doesn't agree with him. Said he'd die for thirty minutes in a hot bubble bath. We knocked, but when you and Mr. Morgan weren't there, and the door was open, I didn't figure you'd mind helping out a sick friend. Finch here said for me to make the cookies. You know, to show how thankful he is."

"I want to talk to him," Gillian said.

"Be kinda hard. Poor guy's dead to the world."

"You know better than this," she said, free hand on her forehead. "You nearly gave me a stroke."

"Sorry. Calm down. Trust me, this place is a total snooze."

"Right," Gillian said, still trying to calm her racing pulse. "Over and out."

"Let's go." Joe's hand was on the door latch.

"Oh, sit down. Didn't you hear a word he said?"

"I don't like it. The whole story…" Joe shook his head. "Something about it's not right."

She sighed. "I agree, it's unconventional, but if you knew Finch, you'd understand. He's the most girly-girl man's man I've ever known. Just married last year, and I swear, he cared more about the caterer, band and flowers than his bride."

Warily eyeing the cookies, Joe joined her at the table. "Those guys were in my house. Without my consent. Cooking. Bathing." He shook his head. "Not only is it not professional, it's a little sick—no, a freakin' *lot* sick."

"I know," she said. "I'm sorry. I'll turn them both in to my supervisor."

Joe pushed back his chair and stood. Grabbed at least five cookies in his left hand, opened the door with his right.

"What are you doing?" she asked, clambering to her feet.

He flung them into the yard. "Cleaning house."

"Yo, BRIMMER, check it out." It was barely seven in the morning when Kavorski waved Brimmer over to the port side of the boat. "This whale looks like it's trying to hump our ride."

"For real?" The sunburned kid with a white streak of zinc oxide on his nose lowered his binoculars to hustle over for a look. "Damn," he said beside Kavorski. "Did I already miss it?"

"Nah. Lean over. There. See it? Don't get too close. That water looks cold enough to be a real nut shrinker."

"Where? You see it right now? God, my niece loves whales. She'll be so jealous if I—"

Kavorski reached under a seat cushion for a .40 caliber SW with a silencer, then shot the kid twice in the back of his head.

With barely a splash, he tipped him over the boat's edge and into rolling blue-green water. The blood made pretty swirls. With any luck, a few sharks would stroll by to finish the job.

"Damn, I'm good." Kavorski gave the kid one last glance, then calmly slipped his piece back under the seat cushion before settling into the captain's chair. "No man wants to deal with the wrath of a jealous woman. Even if she is just your six-year-old niece. One day, Brimmer, you'll thank me for this."

With only two days until his boss's trial, today was also Logue and Mr. Morgan's last.

Tsun-Chung wanted Kavorski and Wesson to wait until dark, but with their only possible witnesses already dead, and a cold front moving in, Kavorski figured what was the point? It was better to just do the job now— in broad daylight. Less chance for Logue or Morgan to escape in the unlikely event something went wrong.

Logue was lucky she'd gotten to play house as long as she did.

It'd been the boss's idea to lull her into believing her part of the whole protection gig was a cakewalk. Then bam—hit her when she least expected it.

They were far enough from the trial that even if somehow the canary escaped, there'd still be time to catch him—then shoot him. And close enough to the trial that the feds' case against Tsun-Chung would be torn to shreds.

Without Joe pointing his finger at Tsun-Chung for the three execution-style shots he'd made to the front of a few too-greedy customs agents' heads, he was squeaky clean. No one but Joe had ever seen him so much as jaywalk.

No one, that is, but his business partners, but they were so well paid, why would any of them be idiot enough to tell?

Every so often, Kavorski thought back to the optimistic kid he'd once been. Full of the Pledge of Allegiance and all that crap. He'd been Captain America. Out to save the day.

Then he'd hit the real world.

Had his wife get cancer without health insurance. Had his son taken by his bitch of a sister-in-law, who'd called him unfit after Carol died. Yeah, well, after his pockets were so full of cash he could hardly walk, they'd see about who made the better parent of the two. They'd just see.

Until then, he had a job to do.

AFTER A SLEEPLESS NIGHT, Gillian was glad for the opportunity to take Bud out for a morning romp. As usual, Joe had wanted to do it, but she'd made him stay inside.

He hadn't liked it.

Any more than she'd liked having to be heavy-handed, but this close to the trial, with this ever-increasing wariness gnawing at her gut, what else could she do?

No matter how many times her partners told her everything on the island was as it should be, every bone in her body said it wasn't.

The day, achingly perfect, with sun-shot diamonds on the water promising warmth, didn't remotely match her cold, edgy mood.

Bud seemed oblivious to her dour vibes. At first, he'd done a considerable bit of "business" on a scraggly cedar. Now he was digging—tail wagging, dirt arcing behind him.

"Hey!" she shouted, heading in his direction. "You wanting another bath?"

Bud kept right on digging.

"What's over there that's so—"

She put her hand over her mouth.

To her left were three dead rabbits. In front of them, a crumbled chocolate chip cookie.

WHEN GILLIAN LEFT, Joe released a long-held breath, telling himself it was good having the place to himself. Whenever she was near, he got this tugging sensation in his stomach. Like he wanted something from her, but wasn't sure what.

For certain, he wouldn't mind a few kisses for the road.

He'd be a liar if he tried denying he wanted more, but that was just chemistry. It didn't come close to explaining the other things going through his head. Like how much he'd like for Meggie to meet Gillian. Get to know her. Enjoy her.

Need her the way Joe did.

He owed Gill an incredible debt. She'd taught him how to laugh again. How to look beyond his pain into a cautiously bright future.

Granted, it wouldn't be the same. Meggie and he would still miss Willow. If he were wholly honest, there was a part of him afraid to be with Meghan because of the memories being around her might drag up. Was there a chance she'd smell of her mother's perfume? Would she have grown to look more like her? Long, golden hair? Pale, creamy skin? A laugh that could sound like delicate, ladylike wind chimes one minute, then transform into pig snorts the next?

He wiped wet eyes.

Grabbed his cereal bowl from the table and stowed it in the sink.

He should've insisted he be the one to walk Bud.

Sitting around here thinking was getting old. Once the trial started, there'd be plenty of time for planning the days and years to come. Would he be greedy for wanting those plans to include both his daughter and Gillian?

Taking a pot out of the cabinet beside the stove, he filled it with water, then set it on the stove to get hot.

Hot.

That about summed up Gillian. Most guys would probably feel lucky in his place—being guarded 24-7 by a woman who looked more like a model than a U.S. Marshal. Wonder if the guys at work constantly hit on her?

The thought had him irrationally pissed.

He and Gillian were friends. Good friends. It was only natural he wouldn't want barrel-chested macho types trying to score. She had better things on her mind. Climbing the marshal ladder—whatever that implied. She didn't have time for dating.

At least not dating anyone beside him.

Whoa.

Waiting for the water to get hot, he paced. Who'd said anything about dating? Just because they'd shared a few kisses didn't mean—

The cabin door flew open, and Bud charged inside.

"Get down!" Gillian shouted, chest heaving. "Guns. Two guys. Maybe three. They—" Still breathing too hard to speak, she bolted the front door, then ran to the cabinet where she'd stashed her radio. She pulled it out and turned it on.

Only there was nothing.

"Shit," she said, knocking it a few times against the counter. The back fell off. Gnawed wires hung like spilled guts.

"Mice," Joe said, not really believing the scene unfolding.

She ran to the bed. Reached under the mattress for the menacing-looking gun that somehow, during the time they'd played house, he'd managed to forget she even had.

From the porch came the clomp of a heavy footstep on the wood planks, then another.

"Get in the back," Gillian said in a stage whisper. "Grab whatever food you can from the pantry. First aid stuff. I'll eliminate this guy, then we'll head cross-country to Wesson and Finch."

Eliminate? As in kill?

Hand to his forehead, Joe froze.

Was this how it had been with Willow the last few minutes of her life? Had her heart pounded? Palms sweated? Had she thought of him the way he was now thinking of…Gillian?

He shook his head to clear it.

This couldn't be happening. He was safe. Gillian was, too. Just like always. Tucked away in his sheltered corner of the world.

"Joe! Snap out of it!" Gillian hissed. "Focus."

He nodded, yet at the same time shook his head.

Gripping his hand, she said, "Look at me, Joe. Right here into my eyes. I promise, I will *never* let anything happen to you. I *will* get you safely home to Meggie. You hear me?"

"Yeah. Sorry. I just—"

"Don't be sorry. Just grab a few supplies, then we're out of here."

The front door latch clicked.

"Go," Gillian whispered. "I've got this under control."

"You going to kill him?"

She nodded. That was what she'd been trained for, wasn't it? What she'd supposedly been waiting for all these years? Real action? Why did the idea sound so repugnant now?

"Don't."

"What do you mean, *don't?* It's not like we have much choice."

He pierced her with a smile of such supreme confidence and calm, it took her breath away. "I've already lost one woman I care about to crazy guys with guns. No way I'm going to lose you, too."

From outside came a muffled male voice. "Thought they were in here, but from the looks of it, they're off on one of their picnics."

Heart pounding, Gillian realized that, from where they stood—in the hall leading to the back door and pantry—they couldn't be seen. From the view through the front windows, the cabin would appear empty.

"Whatever," said another man. "It's an island. Not like they'll get very far."

"Your call. Wanna go hunt 'em down? Or kick the door down and raid the fridge?"

"Christ," Joe said. "If they come in here, then—"

Gillian put her fingers to his lips, then pointed to the hall door he closed on especially cold winter nights. The same door that helped keep the fire's warmth in the living area. Now, the door would buy them a few extra minutes to escape.

While Joe eased the door shut, Gillian shoved as many supplies as she could into a laundry bag hanging from the bathroom wall.

Boom.

Their company was early.

Gillian took a folded stepladder from the pantry, braced it under the hall door.

Boom, boom.

"Ready?" she asked, one hand on the back door, the other reaching out to Joe.

He nodded.

"Let's go. Straight out behind the house. It'll be rough going at first, but—"

"Come on," he said, grabbing her hand for a quick, reassuring squeeze. "I can handle it."

Boom.

They'd just begun their escape when they heard the sound of splintering wood. Hopefully, once inside, the two gunmen would keep busy hunting for snacks.

Outside, Gillian blinked a few seconds in the beating sunshine. It was unseasonably hot. Eerily still.

Their footfalls sounded more like King Kong fleeing the yard than a man and woman. The scent of imminent death magnified each crunch of hiking boot on dirt, each snapped weed or twig.

They'd just made it over the top of the hill when Gillian stopped. "Oh my God, Joe. Bud. Where's Bud?"

Chapter Fourteen

"Great," Joe said. "Of all times for the mutt to run off."

Out of breath, Gillian put her hands on her thighs and groaned.

"What?"

"When I took him out earlier, I had a hard time getting him away from a pretty gruesome find. Took us nearly being shot to get him in the cabin."

"What'd you see?"

"Dead rabbits—three. He was trying to dig up a raccoon carcass. Poor thing looked drained of blood. And that's not the worst. Those rabbits?"

"Yeah?"

"One of those cookies you tossed out the door was nearby—or one of the same batch."

He took a second to let that news sink in, then slapped the trunk of the nearest tree. "Dammit. That mean what I think it does about your pals, Wesson and Finch?"

She swallowed hard. "I can't even imagine guys like them turning to the dark side. Especially not being in cahoots with a lowlife like Tsun-Chung. Surely there's got to be some other explanation."

"Yeah, well, whatever it is, we've got no time to think about it now."

She shot him a sideways glance. "What about Bud?"

"Guess he'll have to fend for himself. We've gotta keep moving."

"You're right," she said with a sharp nod, unable to fathom how much pain Joe's decision to leave his dog had just caused him. "You know the island better than me. Where to?"

"Sea caves," he said without hesitation, turning in that direction.

Gillian followed on his heels, gun at the ready. "What then?"

"Remember when I threatened to haul you back to the mainland in my skiff?"

"Yeah?" she asked while they kept up their pace.

"My boat—she's not exactly seaworthy. I generally keep an outboard here, too, but it's in the shop."

"Not exactly seaworthy?"

"It'll be all right. Assuming you don't mind bailing, and this weather holds, it'll get us where we need to go."

"Swell." She grimaced. "From the mainland, I'll call for backup. Ordinarily, I'd use my cell, but just our luck you picked one of the few spots on the Oregon Coast without a signal."

After a sarcastic grunt, he said, "Up until fifteen minutes ago, that was a good thing."

"Okay, back to business. At this point, we've got to assume everyone else assigned to your case is…"

Though she didn't finish the sentence, Joe stopped to see by her flat expression what she meant. *Dead*. "I keep a car garaged not far from the dock. Maybe it'd be best to drive to L.A.?"

"No," she said, glancing over her shoulder while she took a breather, too. "Portland. There's a marshals' office. My brothers are based out of there."

Joe whistled. "You must really like me, to risk running into them."

"Of all times, you choose now to crack a joke? Joe, this is serious."

"You think?" He cast her a smile. Never had he looked more handsome, even with dirt smudging his left cheek.

"Okay," she admitted with a faint grin. "Probably the dumbest statement I've ever made, but still, me seeing my brothers is nothing compared to getting you back to L.A. in one piece."

"Alive might be good, too."

"Watch it, Morgan. Technically, you don't really need that forked tongue of yours for the trial. Pencil and paper'll work just—"

"Shh…"

From the east came faint sounds of someone walking through heavy brush. "Come on out, kids! It's only a matter of time before this deed is done. Why not finish up early so we can get the hell off this wretched island to go for a nice steak dinner?"

Hunching down, drawing Joe with her, Gillian whispered, "Wesson. I'm guessing he's about three hundred yards away. What do you think?"

"Sounds good. Still think we can make the caves?"

"At this point, that's pretty much our only choice."

Joe led, trying not to make too much noise. Fortunately, the guy looking for them was crashing around so much he provided awesome sound cover.

Bud barked.

Joe froze, as did Gil.

"Get that dog!" Wesson shouted. "It'll make great canary bait!"

"Will do!" This new voice was muffled.

Joe closed his eyes in silent fury. All he'd have to do was call out and Bud would come running. Yet if he did, they'd all die.

One shot rang out.

Two.

Three.

"Damn dog's fast! Like a freakin' rabbit!"

Gillian put her hand on Joe's forearm. Raised her index finger to her lips.

She motioned him up island, away from the caves, but also away from the men. Joe squeezed his eyes shut for a second, thanking God for all those times Bud had run off chasing rabbits. Maybe the mutt had learned a thing or two.

One more shot.

A high-pitched whimper shredded what remained of Joe's heart. This wasn't happening. Couldn't be real.

"Bull's-eye!"

"Dammit, Wesson, you were just supposed to catch him—not kill 'im!"

"Get over it."

"I'm calling the shots here. Don't forget it."

Wesson laughed.

Joe pressed his lips tight. Why was this happening? Was this the point where they took what remained of his life, right down to his dog?

"I want this done clean, Wesson. Weather's supposed to turn into a real nut shrinker by morning, and I'd just as soon not be around for it."

Eyes stinging, Joe wrapped his arms around Gillian, nuzzling the top of her head. She smelled good. Normal. Like they were out for a casual walk instead of running through the woods being chased by guys who shot dogs for sport.

When finally the sound of the men's footfalls and banter faded, Gillian peered up. Her eyes looked big and extra wet.

In some small, stupid way, Joe took comfort in knowing he wouldn't be the only one missing Bud. How was he going to tell Meghan? Maybe this was a sign that he needed to just leave well enough alone where she was concerned. She'd been better off without him all these years, so maybe he should stick with the same routine—assuming he even got off the island.

THEY MADE IT TO THE CAVE.

Tucked beside Joe in the same spot she'd spent her first night on the island, Gillian asked, "How long a walk is it to the boat?"

"Thirty minutes."

"That's not bad."

"For less visibility in case of uninvited guests, I keep it at the abandoned cabin's dock."

She nodded. "Good call. We never saw it."

"Whatever." He wouldn't look at her. Why? She would've liked to see all of his face. To get a feel for how badly he was hurt.

"You hungry?" she asked.

He shook his head.

"Me, neither."

"You should eat," he said.

"But not you?"

"Touché." Still he wouldn't so much as glance her way.

They sat a few minutes in silence, save for the lap of water against rock.

Out of nowhere, Joe said, "You hiding anything else?"

"What do you mean?"

"You didn't tell me about the dead rabbits."

"Are you kidding me?" She sharply laughed. "When was I supposed to tell you? In between gunshots three and four?"

"If that other marshal went bad, how do I know I can trust you?"

"In case you hadn't noticed, those guys were after me, too, Joe. Believe me or not, we're in this together. I swore to protect you, and that's what I'm damn well going to do. I'm sorry I couldn't do the same for Bud, but dammit, as much as I loved the dog, too, I couldn't save him to risk losing you." Tears started. Hot, messy streams down her cheeks. "I—I never had a d-dog. My dad and brothers bought me an ultra-fluffy white cat who did nothing but sit on my bedroom windowsill licking its paws. Whenever I came near it, it hissed. I—I always wanted a great big lovable Lab. He was a good dog, Joe. The best."

She looked up at him, and Joe was lost.

He'd tried pinning the blame on her, believing her capable of such cruelty, but in the end, all it took was one look into her eyes to know she was as innocent as Willow had been.

"I'm sorry," he said, dragging her into his arms. "I don't know why I said that."

"Doesn't matter. I'm tough. I can take it."

"You shouldn't have to."

Exhausted, clinging to this woman he didn't deserve, but had to have, Joe rested his head on hers.

"JOE?" GILLIAN GAVE HIM a nudge. "Wake up. The tide's back down."

He rubbed his eyes, stretched as best he could on the small ledge of sand.

"What time do you think it is?"

"Gotta be after ten with the tide this low."

"How long do you think it'll take to row to town?"

"Two, maybe three hours. We're lucky the water's calm."

"Okay, then that should give plenty of nighttime cover, right?"

"Yeah. Why?"

She drew her bottom lip into her mouth. "Remember the first time Bud got hurt?"

"Kind of hard to forget."

"Right. Well, the past few hours, I've just happened to have a lot of time to hash over a few things. Think back to the first night we spent here. Bud was a pretty big baby, when that cut of his wasn't all that bad."

"So?"

"What if Wesson didn't really kill him? Just grazed him? Bud's soft as they come. What if he just lay down, waiting for one of us to come rescue him? Think you know the island well enough to find him in the dark?"

Joe was instantly wide-awake. "Heck, yeah."

"HE'S NOT HERE."

"Has to be," Joe said in a raised whisper. "I know every inch of this island, and this was the field your *colleague* was standing in when he shot my dog."

"If Bud's not here, then he was at least still alive when…"

They looked for another twenty to thirty minutes with no luck, the whole time getting steadily closer to the cabin.

The generator chugged away, flavoring the night with diesel instead of sweet wood smoke.

Joe clenched his hands, hating to feel so helpless. Like a victim. Again.

He'd had it with this role.

Before stumbling across the drug dealers and murderers that'd ruined his life, he'd never been this kind of loser.

"There." Gil pointed to the cabin porch. "See him?"

Joe looked that way, feeling a surge of hope, followed by defeat, followed by steely determination. Bud. His dog was tied up and miserable-looking on the cabin's cold front porch.

Renewed strength in his every step, Joe headed for the cabin.

"What are you doing?" Gillian yelped, grabbing him

by the back of his T-shirt and tugging him back. "You can't just go storming in there like Rambo."

"Why not? That's what they did to me."

"Joe, please. Be reasonable. You're talking crazy."

"Got a better plan? I'm not leaving without my dog."

Gillian sighed. "Okay, here's what we're going to do…."

"THAT STUPID GENERATOR OUT OF gas again?" Kavorski asked, bologna sandwich to his mouth.

Wesson flicked on a flashlight. "I'll get it."

"Damn right you'll get it," Kavorski said around his latest bite. "If it weren't for you screwing this whole thing up with your little hunting trip, I'd be in a five star hotel right now counting my cash."

"Yeah, yeah, whatever. It's not like they're going anywhere." *Unlike you.* Wesson couldn't wait to get his hands around his so-called partner's throat. Only reason he hadn't already killed him was on the off chance he needed his help.

"They damn well better not go anywhere. It's my ass on the line if they somehow get off this island."

Wesson rolled his eyes.

See? There was the difference between himself and Kavorski. Wesson had long since learned to relax. Savor the moments. He was rather enjoying his game of cat and mouse. Killing was a lot like fine wine. It had to be sipped. Not gulped.

"You know," Wesson said, wrench in hand, imagining all the ways he could use it to kill the man in front of him. "You have real issues when it comes to—"

Ka-boom!

Shards of flying glass from the back door pierced the back of Wesson's head.

While he screamed in fury and pain, Kavorski hit the floor.

"WHERE ARE YOU GOING?" Gillian asked, chasing after Joe on the treacherous trail leading to the ocean. Bud ran in front of him, on the same rope Gillian's traitorous co-workers had used to tie him to the porch.

As she'd hoped, the dog hadn't been badly hurt at all. From the dried blood on his back, she guessed the bullet had grazed him.

"That was such a cinch," Joe said. "I figure why not see if our luck'll hold?"

"Meaning what?" she asked with a hasty check over her shoulder to make sure they weren't being followed.

"Why not ride to the mainland in style?"

"You mean steal Wesson's boat?"

"Heck, yeah. Got a problem with that?"

Gillian groaned. Where did she start? "You think he conveniently left the keys?"

"Worth a shot, isn't it?"

"Logue! Morgan!" Wesson shouted, before firing off three rounds. "You'd better keep running, 'cause when I get hold of you you're beyond dead!"

"Speed it up," Gillian shouted down the trail, awkwardly firing her own weapon into the darkness. "We've got company."

Gillian's lungs burned in agony by the time she joined Joe and Bud in the boat.

As if someone upstairs was smiling on them, Joe had been right: a bundle of silver keys glinted in the moonlight.

"Hold on," he said, turning over the engine and throwing the throttle into reverse.

As a series of shots sparked from shore Gillian fired off four rounds to Wesson's two. "What about the tether ropes?"

"What about 'em?" Joe asked, taking a cleat and a good chunk of the rotten old dock along with them for the ride.

"THIS FEELS WEIRD," Gillian said from the passenger seat of Joe's black Jag. The sumptuous black leather smelled totally different from the island's briny air. The dash was made of some highly polished dark wood inlaid with over a dozen softly glowing panels.

"What?" He didn't take his eyes off the road.

"Hello? After being chased all day and most of the night by gun-toting bad guys, here we are, cruising along in luxury as if nothing happened."

"And…"

"Don't you think we should talk about it? I mean, it's not every day this kind of stuff happens."

He shrugged.

"Think Bud's going to be all right?" They'd left him with Carl—the guy who restocked the cabin—and his wife.

"That dog's going to outlive us all."

Gillian had borrowed Carl's phone to call her boss and fill him in about Wesson. She'd relayed her suspicions about Finch being involved, too, but said she hadn't seen him, and she'd never gotten close enough to recognize the other man working with Wesson. She also was unsure of the whereabouts of Kavorski or Brimmer.

William Benton told her to lie low, then promised to send someone to get them, along with arranging for local authorities to clean up the mess they'd left on the island. She'd mustered every ounce of courage to tell him thanks for the offer of finding them a ride, but no thanks. That just to be safe, she'd get Joe to the Portland marshals' office. William reluctantly agreed.

While she'd been on the phone, she'd seen Joe hand Carl a large wad of cash, then ask him to keep an eye on the dog for the next few weeks. When Carl had asked where Joe would be, he'd said something had come up.

Joe, in no frame of mind to talk, turned on the radio, settling for a classical station he hoped would put Gillian to sleep. On one of their picnics, she'd mentioned being a fan of alternative rock.

Within ten minutes, she was out, leaving him alone with his thoughts. A place he now wasn't so certain he wanted to be.

Pretty amazing how much had gone down back on the island. But at the same time, inside him, how little had changed. Here he was, yet again running scared.

After the trial, would that change? Would his repeat testimony finally bring an end to his running?

God, he missed his little girl.

Hearing her laugh over cartoons while he sat at the breakfast table, drinking fresh-squeezed orange juice and reading the *Wall Street Journal*. Willow slept late, then stayed late at the office, so morning had been his time with Meggie. Sometimes he'd actually get her to eat a breakfast more substantial than Pop Tarts.

The night before, Willow would carefully lay out the clothes Meggie was supposed to wear to preschool, but he and his daughter had always secretly jazzed up those outfits. Making additions like a pirate eye patch or pom-poms or a tiara.

All the way to school, they'd sing commercial jingles, neither of them remembering the real words. By the time they arrived, Joe never wanted to let her go.

And so sometimes they'd drive around a little more.

To the doughnut shop at the end of Lever Road for cake doughnuts with pink sprinkles. Did she still like those? Or were her tastes more refined now that she was a Beverly Hills kid? Was she more into croissants?

On and on into the night he drove.

He pulled over to gas up, and once back on the road, Gillian again fell asleep. Portland wasn't that far from his island. He could've been there and back twice. But it felt good being behind the wheel. Like he was back in control.

But then he made the mistake of looking at the woman sleeping beside him. And never had he felt more *out* of control.

Chapter Fifteen

"Where are we?" Gillian asked, shivering in the chilly night air Joe had let in upon entering the car.

"A cheap motel. Apparently the only kind out in the middle of nowhere." He handed her a single brass key dangling from a burgundy plastic diamond key chain.

"Classy," she said with a weary grin.

"Hey, only the best for the women I date." He leaned over and kissed her cheek.

She wanted to be excited by his playful words, but as tired as he had to be, as unconventional as their situation, she knew those words meant nothing more than a faint stab at lightening their moods.

"The place only has rooms with one bed," he said. "That okay?"

She nodded.

He started the car, driving it to the far end of the single story motel, which looked suspiciously like the one used in Psycho.

He parked behind a Dumpster so the car wouldn't be visible from the road.

"Want me to call the bellman to fetch our bags?" she asked.

"Ha ha." He climbed out, walked around to her side as if he planned on opening her door, but she'd already done it.

She handed him the room key.

Inside, he flicked on a lamp that sat on a low table between two gold velvet chairs. Gold-flecked wallpaper served as a lovely backdrop to the gold brocade bed. Stale cigarette smoke filled the air, but never had Gillian felt more secure. No way was anyone finding them here.

She jumped when Joe tossed the key on the dresser with a clang.

"It's okay," he said, curving his hands around her shoulders. "Well…" Slowly turning her to face him, he added, "Aside from the sixties-era James Bond decor, it's okay."

Easing her arms around him for a hug, she said, "Thanks, but aren't I supposed to be reassuring you?"

"Sorry. I forgot. Have at it."

She gave him a swat, then reached for the remote. They got a whole six channels. Two aired church services, one news, one infomercials, one *Love Boat*, one *Gunsmoke*. In the mood for entertainment that didn't include gunplay, she backed onto the too-soft bed, settling for watching Cruise Director Julie fall in love.

"Mind if I take a shower?" Joe asked.

"Go ahead. Sounds like a good idea."

He reached into the laundry bag and pulled out a sack.

"What's in there?"

"Toothbrushes and paste. A couple T-shirts for us to change into. I grabbed them while you were in the restroom at the gas stop." One shirt was gray and featured six Oregon lighthouses. The second was navy with a baby seal. "This one's for you," he said, handing her the navy one. "As much as I'd love seeing you in a color other than blue, I figured you'd feel more at home in this."

"Thanks." His sweet gesture tightened her throat.

"Got some junk food, too." He tossed bags of beef jerky and Doritos on the bed, along with two packs of powdered sugar doughnuts, Pringles and a couple of Snickers. "Hmm…" Eyeing his selections, he said, "All this looked better a hundred miles back. Now I'd prefer your French toast." He winked, only something about the seemingly casual gesture wasn't right. The way he stood there, hands in his pockets, outwardly so calm when on the inside he had to be freaking out… Was he putting on this ultrarelaxed act for her?

"I—I like all this stuff," she said, avoiding the real issue. If one of her co-workers had turned dirty, what if others had, too? Was the Portland office even safe? What happened if they got vibes that it wasn't? Then what? They couldn't keep running forever. Should she turn Joe over to the LAPD?

He jerked his thumb toward the bathroom. "I'm heading for the shower."

"Joe, wait."

"What?"

"Don't you think we should talk?"

"About what?"

"Everything. My God, we both could've been killed. And it's all my fault."

Silently, stoically, he crossed the room, settled his big hands on either side of her face, then slowly drew her up.

"No. It's not," was all he said before tipping her face sideways, then covering her mouth with his.

He kissed her urgently, sweetly, with such raw emotion her heart begged him to stop, while at the same time go on forever. Did he know what this did to her?

It gave her false hopes of them having a future beyond the coming days and weeks. It made her want things she'd long since considered taboo. Things like little girls named Meggie, and babies, and two-story Victorians, and formal Sunday dinners around a dining room table busting with people she loved. Only none of that was ever going to happen for her, because she didn't want it to, right? Those were things her father and brothers wanted for her, not what she wanted down deep in her soul….

Which, at the moment, consisted solely of Joe kissing her and kissing her until the world stopped spinning.

He pulled back. Sighed. "Time for that shower. Cold."

"Joe…"

"If I don't go…"

Forcing back tears, she nodded.

If he didn't go, who knew where kisses could lead?

Hugging herself while he entered the bathroom, flicked on the noisy fan-light, then shut the door, she couldn't help but wonder where he wanted their kissing to lead.

If he hadn't still been mourning Willow, if she hadn't been bound by a professional code of honor to keep her hands to herself, how different would things be between them? Would he be a romantic? Courting her over candlelight? Or the outdoorsy type? Preferring sailing or canoeing or—

She sat down as hard as the mushy mattress allowed.

Who was she trying to kid?

Code of honor? She snorted. She'd thrown that out the window days ago. Face it, if she hadn't fallen for the guy, he never would've been in danger. She'd have kept her radio and gun close at hand instead of tucked into some mouse-infested cabinet. She'd have followed up on that gnawing feeling that something had been wrong. She'd have focused on all those suspicions instead of trying to figure out names for the exact shade of Joe's eyes and hair.

If it weren't for his quick thinking in taking a chance on finding the keys in Wesson's boat, they'd both be dead. She was assigned to protect him, yet he'd been the one who'd ultimately got them to safety. He'd driven through the night while she'd used his shoulder for a pillow.

Boy, was that cause for a promotion, or what?

Laughing, crying, she withdrew her silver star from her jacket pocket and set it on the bedside table.

Her father and brothers had been right. She made a lousy marshal. Who had she been trying to kid?

Desperate to feel something—anything—besides the pain stemming from realizing her life's goal was a joke, she peeled off her clothes.

Easing open the bathroom door, she stood there for a second, breathing in the faint smell of disinfectant and the steam.

"Gil?" Joe asked from the shower.

"Uh-huh."

"You needing the john?"

"No."

"Then what…" He peeked his head around the shower curtain, then openly stared. "Oh."

Closing the door, she crossed the small space to join him. "I—I didn't want to be alone."

When she put her hands on his chest, easing her fingertips through the coarse, wet hair, she had a front row ticket to the erratic pulse in his throat. She pressed open-mouthed kisses to his pecs, slid lower to his nipples and lower still to an area standing at attention.

"God," he moaned, tilting his head back. "Stop. I'll never last."

"No one's asking you to," she said, easing him back so she could join him under the sinfully hot spray. She went back to giving him pleasure, and he didn't last, and so she washed him, and he grabbed the soap and washed her. Only they never made it to the rinse portion, as not three minutes after she began rhythmically rubbing against him he was hard again and the water was growing cold.

"Let's get out of here," he said, turning off the faucet, then flinging back the curtain.

He hefted her into his arms, kissing her lips, cheeks, neck, setting her down long enough to rip the spread off the bed. But in the split second it took him to do that, she grew tired of waiting, and pulled him back, twining her arms around his neck, kissing the indentation at the base of his throat.

He slipped his strong fingers under the fall of her hair,

lightly tugging back her head, roughly seizing her mouth, parting it to allow for the primal thrusting of their tongues.

Shower droplets made way for sweat.

The pocket between her legs hummed, and she eased them apart, urging one, and then two of his fingers inside her. When his rhythmic plunging had pushed her over the edge of reason, she tugged him down to the bed, inviting him in, only the bed was too soft and she'd sunk into it too far.

"Dammit," he said while she giggled. "Think this is funny?"

"Uh-huh."

"Okay, then, let's try this...." He took her hand, guiding her to the nearest wall. Leaning against it, he drew her again into the circle of his arms, into the warm shelter she so badly craved. He was kissing her, and then lifting her up, up, only to plunge deep within her.

At first all she could do was gasp, but then with his every thrust, she pressed her fingertips into his back, kissing his shoulders, nipping his neck, until he ducked low to once again claim her lips, dizzying her with bold sweeps of his tongue.

A few more deep, binding, soul-shattering thrusts and he tensed, while she clung to him, scarcely able to breathe past an all-consuming, shimmering white-hot glow.

"Thank you," he said, pressing a tender kiss to her forehead.

"Thank *you*."

Back on her feet, she held out her hand. "Think the water's warm yet?"

"Don't know," he said, twining his fingers with hers. "Let's see."

JOE WOKE THE NEXT MORNING, took one look at the woman lying beside him, and felt like the biggest womanizing jerk to ever live. Slipping his arm out from under her, he headed for the bathroom, rinsed off in what had to be his fourth or fifth shower in the last twelve hours, then dressed in dirty jeans and his new butt-ugly T-shirt.

He wanted to go outside. Fill his foggy brain with fresh air. But even though the odds that they'd been followed were slim, taking a stroll didn't seem like all that bright an idea.

Settling for sitting in a ratty gold chair that had a cushion about as played out as the bed, he swiped his fingers through his damp hair.

Okay, where did he even begin sorting all this out?

First step was taking another look at Gil.

God, she was beautiful, but her looks had never been up for debate. Her long hair was bunched around her face, looking more like a hat than sleek and sexy, but that was okay. She could've have been bald and he suspected he'd still have a raging boner for the woman. Leading him back to the whole chemistry issue.

For all practical purposes, he was taken. Sure, Willow had been dead for, like, two years, but that didn't make the pain easier to bear. The only thing that did that was…Gillian.

Talking with Gillian, laughing with Gillian.

Having wild-ass, kinky shower sex with Gillian—the kind you sure didn't have with your wife.

Great. So what did that mean? That she meant nothing more to him than a one-night stand? Because that wasn't the case at all. When he dared take a glimpse at his future, he couldn't imagine life without her in it.

What if Meggie turned him down cold? Said she didn't want to get to know a dad who'd for all practical purposes abandoned her? If that happened, the only possible person he could talk it over with was Gillian.

He grabbed a Snickers off the table and tore open the wrapper with his teeth.

His mouth still tasted like her.

He took a big bite of the candy bar and chewed.

Bottom line, whatever was going down between them had to end. Today. Now.

He no right to take things further.

Not the faintest idea even how.

He was too old for dating. Too tired for the games. He only wished he was too old and tired for the want-ing. Even now, after giving himself the well-intentioned speech, he wanted her. Wanted her just as keenly as the first day he'd eyed her walking on his shore.

"YOU ALL RIGHT?" Gillian was back in the Jag's pas-senger seat, only this time, she'd propped her sock-cov-ered feet on the dash. If he'd seemed to mind, she'd have put them down, but since trading their motel room that'd looked so cozy in the darkness, yet so shabby in glar-ing morning light, for an equally blah cold, gray day, he'd hardly paid her any attention at all.

He drove with both hands on the wheel. Narrowed eyes and a grimly held mouth weren't exactly what she would've hoped for the morning after from the man who'd made love to her all night.

Appropriate, maybe, considering their circumstances, but not welcome.

What she wanted was the laughter they'd shared back on the island. Playing pick-up sticks late at night or reading each other passages from books they'd been immersed in.

"Just thinking," he said in answer to the question she'd forgotten having asked. "Wonder what we're about to run into?"

She squeezed her eyes shut.

What had she expected? For him to be thinking of her? Remembering what her hands, her mouth, had felt like on him, the way her mind kept replaying the feel of his rough fingers along her collarbone and throat?

From the state highway leading out of Corvallis, he hit the northbound ramp for I-5. "Are there going to be feds everywhere? Are they going to lock me up like some freakin' alien?"

"Don't think of being protected as being jailed. When it's over, and you're back with… Meggie, it'll be worth it."

"Yeah. Guess you're right."

"Sure I am." She shot a lazy smile his way. One that if they'd been real lovers she'd have followed up with reaching for his right hand, lacing her fingers with his and giving him a gentle squeeze. But the fact of the matter was they weren't lovers. They were barely friends. For all practical purposes, they were nothing. Just business acquaintances who'd shared time together.

If only she believed that in her heart. Maybe then she wouldn't be faced with the superhuman task she knew—for Joe's safety and her own conscience—had to be done.

Chapter Sixteen

"Logue!" her team leader, Neil Kavorski, shouted through an open office door. "I'll be doggoned, get the hell in here, girl! I can't believe you're all right."

Gillian initially shied away from him, but he made it impossible by pulling her into a hug. How had he survived? Hadn't Wesson killed everyone else on their team? Or for that matter, could Kavorski have been secretly working with Wesson?

Her stomach turned queasy until she stepped back and saw the cuts across his left cheek, bruises on his forehead and jaw.

"Sorry about that," he said, blushing after their hug. "Guess touchy-feely stuff isn't exactly professional, but hell, I'm just so damn relieved to see you in one piece. We've all been worried sick. Some shock about Wesson and Finch going bad, huh? God, when Wesson came at me with his Maglite, knocked me out, shot young Brimmer…it was all so fast! I didn't know what was happening. When I came to, I radioed for help, but then I saw an explosion up at the cabin and thought I was too late."

He shook his head. "Anyway, Finch is still missing and Wesson is dead."

"How?" Gillian asked, in regard to Wesson's death.

"Found him dead on the trail leading up to the cabin. Shot in the chest."

On the trail?

Gillian squeezed her eyes shut, forcing down a hot rush of nausea. Did that mean one of those shots she'd blindly fired into the night had killed him?

"Good aim," Kavorski said, patting her back. "Ballistics showed it had to be your weapon that did the job. So?" he asked, glancing beyond her to the bustling outer office. "Don't suppose you have our witness with you?"

"I wanted to check things out first. Make sure it was safe."

"Sure." There he was again with the back patting. In all the years she'd worked with the guy, he'd never come within five feet of her. "Smart. I always knew you were one of those brainiac types. Damn fine marshal, too."

Grimacing, she said, "Thanks, but—"

"No, really." He ushered her into a chair in a loaner office and shut the door. "Will Benton and me were just talking after the debriefing about what a long way you've come. Met your brothers this morning. They all seemed like good guys. Real proud of you—all three of 'em."

She looked down, fingered the brass name plaque on Kavorski's temporary desk. The man's ego was so big, he took the stupid thing with him wherever he happened to land. She'd always looked down on him for that. But seeing how far she'd fallen in such a short amount of time, she was the last one who should be casting stones.

"There's talk of you landing a promotion for this," he said. "Yep, you've made every last one of us proud."

Gillian's stomach roiled. How was she going to do it? Quit the job she loved at the very office where Caleb, Adam and Beau were based? Yet she had to. It was the right thing. She'd broken the rules in a very big way. Not only was she no longer fit to protect Joe, but her head was hardly in the right place. Not after last night. Not after she'd known him in ways she'd never known any man.

"I told—"

"Look, Kavorski," she sighed. "I appreciate your support, but I want off Joe's…" She cleared her throat. "Mr. Morgan's case. In fact, as soon as I can get to a computer, I'll be turning in my resignation."

"What?"

"I crossed a few lines, and—"

He looked to his desk. Picked up a jumbo pack of Juicy Fruit. He pulled out a stick and offered it to her.

"No, thanks."

He took his time unwrapping it, popped it in his mouth and chewed. The sweet smell made it all the way to her and did nothing for her already upset stomach. "Brimmer and I saw you holding hands once—with Mr. Morgan. I'd hoped you were just showing support, but I'm assuming it went a little further?"

She crossed her legs. "I need out. Let's just leave it at that." Withdrawing her star from her pocket, the star she'd worked so hard for, dreamed her whole life of earning, she set it on Kavorski's desk.

Her throat hurt as bad as if she'd come down with a wicked case of strep. Her eyes stung.

I will not cry. I will not cry.

"Listen," he said, voice uncharacteristically sympathetic. "Nothing about this case has been routine. Maybe the higher-ups will cut you some slack. In the meantime, transfer Mr. Morgan to my custody and I'll take it from there. You just relax. Take a few bubble baths—whatever it is you chicks do to chill."

"Shouldn't we get Mr. Benton in on this, too? I mean, there's gotta be paperwork. My own debriefing."

Kavorski waved her off, gave her another pat on her back. "God knows you've already been through enough. I can't even imagine how tough it must've been for you getting Morgan off that island." He laughed. "Christ, all I did was lay there passed out on my boat, but you—you're a freakin' hero."

Yeah. Some hero, sleeping with the man she'd sworn to protect.

"Where is he?" Kavorski pressed. "Mr. Morgan?"

"Joe? He's at a coffee house down the street. Three exits. Nice size crowd."

"Sounds good. You're a bright girl, Logue. I'm going to miss you. Maybe when we all get back to L.A., we can change your mind about leaving the family."

I'm not going to cry. I will not cry. "I, um, don't think so. But thanks for the thought."

"All right, then, let me just grab a coat—that rain up here's a coldhearted bitch."

Hurry, Gillian's heart said with each frantic beat. Even more than she wanted to get on with the business of saying goodbye to Joe, she wanted out of this office before running into one—or all—of her brothers. Turning her star in to Kavorski was one thing. Handing it over to one of their told-you-so faces was unthinkable.

SITTING STIFFLY across the table from Gillian, listening to his next babysitter, Kavorski, prattle on, knowing he was only minutes from saying goodbye, Joe realized he hadn't experienced such a profound sense of loss since losing Willow.

But that was nuts. He barely knew Gillian, and Willow had been his wife.

"Yep, this place holds a lot of memories," Kavorski said. "I was working a case up here in the eighties—had more hair back then," he said, rubbing his bald head. "Doug Ash was top dog. Poor schmuck. Wife left him for a gym teacher 'cause she said Doug didn't spend enough time with her. So anyway, to try and make him feel better, me and some of the guys decided to set him up on a blind date, so…"

Joe gazed past Kavorski to Gillian.

Look at her.

Sitting there enraptured, as if this guy was actually entertaining instead of boring as hell. Was that her way of telling him their lovemaking had meant nothing? That he'd just been a little action on an otherwise dull night?

He didn't believe it.

Couldn't believe it.

But he had to.

Kavorski bottomed-up his coffee. Glanced at his watch. "Guess we'd better get this show on the road," he said to Joe. "We've got a lot of miles to get under our belts if we want to hit L.A. tomorrow. We could fly, but

I'd feel better keeping John Q. Public out of this. If Tsun-Chung found out you were on a flight and blew the whole thing just to get to you…" Shaking his head, he tsked-tsked.

"Sure," Joe said. "Whatever you say."

At this point, he didn't care. Whether he flew, drove or took a wagon train to the trial, he just wanted the damn thing over with so he could once and for all get on with his life. He couldn't wait to get back to his daughter. To normalcy.

Life with Gillian had been a lot of things, but normal wasn't one of them. Happy. Sad. A constant hard-on. How the hell was he now supposed to just say goodbye?

"Um, see ya." She held out her hand. The same small hand that had run up and down his back, digging her fingertips into his naked—

He set out to return her polite handshake, but ended up dragging her into a hug. Oh, she might not have wanted to, but she hugged him back.

Fiercely, protectively, as though she cared for him, too. Something true that, if only they'd met under different circumstances at a different time, they might have built upon.

"I—I'll miss you," she said, standing on her tiptoes, her voice raspy and her breath warm in his ear. "Please watch out for yourself. Be careful who you trust."

"You, too," he said, letting her go quickly before he didn't just drag her into another hug, but into Kavorski's car along with them.

GILLIAN HAD FLOWN into Portland, leaving her without a ride. On their way to town this morning, Joe had asked if she wanted to drive his car back to L.A. for him, but she'd politely turned him down.

Too messy.

It would necessitate another goodbye.

Careful not to look in the direction Kavorski had taken Joe, she returned to her team's temporary offices to grab her few personal belongs. Her purse and cell phone. She had sixty-seven bucks and change. Surely that'd be enough to get her to the airport.

She'd almost made a clean getaway when a male voice called out from behind her, "Gilly? That you?"

Caleb. Her oldest brother. Biggest pain in her neck.

Groaning, she weighed her options. Run? Hide? Pretend to only be impersonating Gillian Logue? All sounded better than what she ended up doing, which was turning around to face him. "Hey. Long time no see."

"Hey? That the best you can do?" He crushed her in a hug. "Dad's a mess. Hell, we all are. Why didn't you tell us you were coming? Dammit, Gillian, the only way we even found out you were in trouble was through a courtesy call from your boss. He said you didn't want anyone knowing where you were."

"True," she said, squirming out of his arms.

"Why? One of us—shoot, all of us—could've gone out to that island with you. Protected you."

That did it. Enough polite chit-chat.

She was out of there.

Chin raised, she said, "The last thing I need from you, Caleb, is protecting. In case you hadn't noticed, I grew up. Then somehow, without any of my big brothers' help, I managed to bring Joe Morgan in safely all on my own."

Caleb rolled his eyes. "Lighten up, Gillybug. You know I didn't mean it like that."

Gillybug?

He hadn't called her that since she was nine years old and he was helping her into a ladybug costume she'd worn in a Marcus C. Webster Elementary School play.

She turned her back on him to leave, but just like always, he was faster. Yanking her by the sleeve of the navy marshal jacket she'd fought so hard to wear and now had to give up, he said, "You're acting like a spoiled brat. If you've got any downtime before heading back to L.A., I'm sure Dad would appreciate a visit. He misses you—the *real* you."

"And I suppose you, better than anyone, knows who the real me is?"

"Used to." Shaking his head, he said, "Now I doubt anyone—especially you—has a clue."

HOURS LATER, on a park bench, sitting ramrod straight despite a steady cold rain, Gillian figured she couldn't have screwed up her life more if she'd tried. After finally being giving the assignment that would jump-start her career, finally make everyone from her father to her brothers to her chauvinistic co-workers see she was every bit as good at her job as any man, she'd had to go and blow it by falling in love.

How could she have been so stupid?

It was like some cornball female cliché.

She didn't want to be in love. Before now, wasn't even sure she'd known what love was. Sure, she'd had a strong affection for Kent, but that hadn't been the same. What she felt for Joe was different. Deeper.

How she'd finally accepted the fact that it had to be love turning her life upside down was in realizing she'd willingly do it all again. Lose her job. Her reputation. Shoot, her sanity, all for just one more night in Joe's arms. What else could cause that degree of havoc but love?

THIRTY MINUTES DOWN I-5, Kavorski asked, "Need a snack or anything? Bathroom break?"

"I'm good," Joe said, staring out the government-issued sedan's rain-streaked window. In the time they'd been on the road, clouds had turned into drizzle, which had turned into a soaking the likes of which he hadn't seen since the day Gillian had first shown up on his island.

Where was she now?

What was she doing?

Thinking about him the way he couldn't stop thinking about her?

"Yep." Kavorski fiddled with the radio dial. Settled on a grating country song. "I ever tell you about the time me and my good pal Frank came fishing up here? Well, it was raining just about like this, and damn, but it was colder than a witch's titty in a brass bra. I'm talking a real nut shrinker. Anyway, we got this old boy to take us out, and we were just—"

"Would you mind saving this for another time? I could use some shut-eye." Joe closed his eyes, but more as a deterrent to his driver than because he thought for one second he'd actually be able to sleep.

God, the guy's voice was annoying. Familiar, too.

Joe straightened in his seat. Glanced Kavorski's way, trying to place him. Had he been in the safe house last go-around?

"Yeah, speaking of nut shrinkers," Kavorski said, "I ever tell you 'bout the time I was up here hunting and it started to snow…."

This time, Joe let him ramble on, trying, trying to place him. The more he listened, the more he got the impression the guy wasn't just talking to be friendly. He seemed nervous. Like he was trying to cover for something. Despite all his talk of nut-shrinking cold weather, a faint sheen of sweat had broken out on his forehead.

Please watch out for yourself. Be careful who you trust.

Gillian's last words rang in Joe's ears. He focused on the meaning behind them, not the fact that he'd been turned on by the notion she still cared.

Be careful who you trust.

Had she been trying to tell him something between the lines? That even though she was placing his life in this guy's hands, she didn't completely trust him? Or was it some of the other marshals he'd come in contact with she didn't trust?

"…And man, let me tell you, was it cold. I'd tell you it was a nut shrinker of a day, but you've probably already guessed that. So me and my friend Frank—he's the same one I go fishing with—we…"

The guy sure was preoccupied with weather. Especially cold weather—and his nuts.

I want this done clean, Wesson. Weather's supposed to turn into a real nut shrinker by morning, and I'd just as soon not be around for it.

"…Frank took off runnin'. Geez Louise. I've never seen a grown man run that fast. Looked like a—what's the matter, Mr. Morgan? You're looking green. Carsick?"

Trying to act calm, even though he was in a car doing seventy with one of the guys who'd just tried killing him back on his island, Joe said, "Now that you mention it, I am feeling like I might retch. Mind pulling over at the next exit for Dramamine?"

"Will do," Kavorski said, turning up the radio, humming along with the tune. "Oh yeah, where was I? Oh—Frank's running…."

It took fifteen minutes to get to the next exit.

Unbearable minutes during which Joe's pulse raged so loud in his ears he worried Kavorski might hear. But then how could he over his own drone?

"…It was the damnedest thing, seeing him with his arm out like that. Just sort of flopping. But then, shoot, I suppose…"

Think, Joe, think.

If only Gillian were here. She'd know what to do. She'd been trained for this sort of thing. She'd gone on and on about what a poor job she'd done, but even about old Kavorski here, she must've had an innate suspicion something hadn't been right.

"This place float your boat?" Kavorski asked, pulling into the gravel lot of the Jug & Lug.

"Sure." Joe's mouth had gone so dry it was hard uttering even the one word. *Normal.* He had to appear as if everything was normal.

Kavorski parked the sedan. The sound of the tires crunching to a stop was deafening. Joe's every sense was on full alert.

"Don't know about you," Kavorski said, exiting the car to step through a light drizzle, then pocketing the keys. "But I could use a stiff drink. Been a wild few days, hasn't it?"

"Yep." *Few days?* For Joe, it had only been the past twenty-four hours that'd been especially rough—comparatively speaking. After losing his wife, the quality of his days had been judged on a different scale. One topped by times he'd pushed himself to such physical exhaustion he was incapable of calculating where all he'd gone wrong.

But then Gillian had shown up. Changed everything.

Before her, truth was, he might not have cared if Kavorski shot him dead. But now he did care. He had to get back to Meggie, and though he might not have realized it until this very minute, he had to get back to Gillian. To try making sense of his mixed-up feelings where she was concerned.

Kavorski yawned. Belched. "S'cuse me. Must've had one too many pieces of cold pizza for lunch."

"Go right ahead," Joe said with a big smile. "Men gotta be men, I always say."

"I knew I liked you." Kavorski laughed, holding open the convenience store door. "That coffee we had back in town running right through you the way it is me?"

"You know it."

Kavorski gave the clerk a tight wave, then led the way through a maze of aisles selling everything from candy bars to tampons to motor oil. The men's room was all the way at the back.

"Beauty before brains," Kavorski said, standing beside the open door to the one-seater restroom.

Joe managed a laugh.

In the bathroom, he shut and locked the door. He was too panicked to pee, so he instead searched for a weapon.

Paper towels.

Scummy bar soap.

Air freshener on the back of the john promising alpine freshness.

Plunger.

In case Kavorski was paying attention, Joe flushed. He then lurched for the plunger.

He stepped on the red rubber tip, pulling it off with the bottom of his hiking boot, then kicked it behind the john. The handle, he shoved down the waistband of his jeans, working it down the length of his leg.

Again for Kavorski, he turned on the faucet, swiped his hands under the water's cool flow, then splashed his face.

He grabbed a towel, dried himself, then took a deep breath.

Chapter Seventeen

"TOOK YOU LONG ENOUGH," Kavorski said, brushing past Joe and into the bathroom. "Hang tight. I'll be right back."

"Will do."

After Kavorski closed the door, Joe took out his makeshift club. Held it behind him.

"Find everything you need?" The clerk, a pretty red-head with kinky curly hair, pushed a dry mop across the floor.

Joe's pulse hammered. Great. He didn't want anyone but Kavorski getting hurt. If Kavorski pulled out a gun—no. He wasn't even going to think of what all could go wrong. Just what could go right.

Gillian and Meggie both, back in his arms.

That was the ultimate end goal.

He smiled and nodded in the woman's direction.

She mopped her way over to a chip stand.

From in the bathroom came the whoosh of the toilet flushing. Was Kavorski the type who washed his hands?

Nope. He fumbled through the door and then—wham!

Joe hit him once, twice across the back of his head.

The marshal crumpled to the floor before he could even see who or what had struck him.

Violently shaking, Joe knelt beside the man, fishing in his pockets for the keys. He stood, only to find the clerk staring.

"Please don't kill me." She started to cry, fell to her knees. "I've got kids. A baby and a three-year-old. I'll show you pictures. *Please.*"

"Stop crying," he said. "This isn't what you think. He's the bad guy. Got anywhere I could lock him up while you call the police?"

Hand trembling, she pointed toward a walk-in cooler. On the outside of a huge stainless steel door hung an open padlock. Perfect.

Teeth gritted, Joe dragged Kavorski inside.

The space was cold, but not a true "nut shrinker." Should suit Kavorski just fine. Joe didn't bother turning on the overhead light. Just shut the door, then rammed home the lock.

Leaning against cool metal, hands braced on his knees, he felt relief shimmer through him. Hot and cold all at once, Exhilarated, yet like he might throw up.

"P-please don't kill me," the woman with the mop said again.

"You call the cops yet?"

She shook her head.

"You might want to. When this guy wakes, he's not going to be happy."

"W-what s-should I say?"

"Got a pen and paper?"

GILLIAN'S FLIGHT TO L.A. left in an hour, time she was passing reading the newspaper while downing a tasteless rubber cheeseburger she'd bought at an airport restaurant.

She squeezed more ketchup on it, trying to taste something, feel something—even if it was revulsion.

Ever since saying goodbye to Joe, since beginning the first minutes of her life without him, she'd felt numb.

Maybe she should've at least stayed with her job until Joe was safely back in L.A.? The odds were slim, but what if Kavorski was dirty, too? Who had been that other guy with Wesson? It hadn't been Finch. From a distance, she'd heard the guy talk, but his voice hadn't seemed familiar. She'd been on the radio with Kavorski all week. Surely she'd have recognized his tone if that had indeed been him? Or had the usually static-filled radio distorted his voice to an unrecognizable degree?

Even if she had broken her code of honor, she should've insisted on staying with Joe. She could've protected him with an even higher code—a code of love.

She nearly choked on her latest bite.

This was stupid. The what-ifs. The worrying. It wouldn't help anything. Even if Joe was in trouble, she was hardly the one he'd want to turn to for—

Her cell rang.

Her heart lurched.

Joe? In her dreams. He didn't even have the number. "Hello?"

"Gillian?" Her boss. Will Benton. "We've got trouble."

WHERE COULD HE BE?

Gillian had been driving the I-5 for hours, careening in a rental car up and down the interstate where Joe and Kavorski had last been seen.

She'd returned to Bayside, spoken to Carl and his wife. Neither of them had seen Joe. From the worry on their faces, she never once thought they were lying.

Would he have rented a boat to get back out to the island? But why? It wasn't as if he had a cabin to return to.

Carl's wife had insisted Gillian looked tired, then plied her with coffee and lemon Bundt cake. Bud had licked her to within an inch of her life.

It'd felt good knowing at least one of the Morgan men missed her.

She called her boss again, but he still had no news other than that Kavorski had been taken into police custody pending further investigation into what'd gone down on the island.

One point Gillian had been relieved about—Kavorski had lied about ballistics proving her gun had shot Wesson. Actually, it'd been his. Brimmer and Finch were still officially missing, though Gillian feared the worst for the two young men.

Poor Rachel, Finch's new bride. She must be crazed with worry.

Tsun-Chung's trial was due to start in the morning. Without their star witness, the prosecution was pushing for a continuance. The defense was pushing for full speed ahead. Or better yet, a dismissal.

Back in her car, driving aimlessly up the coast, Gillian pulled into the lot of an abandoned warehouse, turned off her car, then thumped her forehead against the wheel.

Could she have possibly messed this up any worse?

At least Joe was alive, but what if the bad guys found him again? What if he went and did something crazy, like instead of driving to the nearest police station and turning himself in, he pulled another disappearing act? She'd be solely to blame. For coming on to him. For being just like her brothers and father had said—not strong enough, not capable enough to do her job.

If Joe vanished again, not only would the drug lord go free, but what about Meggie? She'd never again know what it was like having a dad.

Tears started and they didn't show signs of letting up.

Gillian cried for the little girl she'd never even met. For the man she hadn't even begun to know as well as she'd like.

What should she do? There had to be something she hadn't thought of. Something she wouldn't ordinarily do.

There were lots of things.

Playing in traffic. Chewing with her mouth open. Talking to strangers. Shoot, for the most part, she was a pretty safe girl. Not that her brothers and father ever thought so. They'd just as soon lock her in an injury-proof dollhouse, where she'd never again do anything by herself.

By herself...

That was it! The one thing she'd never do was ask for help, but in this case, she'd run out of options. As much as it would personally destroy her, when it came to finding Joe, she'd do anything—even if that meant going back to her childhood home to admit the one thing she'd never thought she would. As her dad and brothers had always said, she didn't have what it took to be a U.S. Marshal.

"THAT'S MY GIRL," Vince Logue said, shaking his head and smiling. "I always knew she'd make me proud."

"Refill?" Adam Logue, Gillian's youngest brother held a coffeepot over Joe's mug.

"No, thanks," Joe said. "I'm about to float away as it is." He'd been in the Logues' kitchen for over two hours, having driven straight there after knocking out Kavorski. He might be a lot of things—stubborn, pig-headed and proud—but he wasn't stupid. He knew when he was in over his head.

Minutes after leaving the convenience store, he'd formed a mental short list of the people in his life he could trust. Gillian topped the list, followed by the men who'd raised her in the small town of Desolation Point. Sure, she'd gone on about how she'd lived her whole life trying to get away from them, but Joe saw her situation from a different perspective. He saw her for the smart, funny, accomplished miracle she was. He could only hope one day she'd see herself the same way he did.

"Pops," Gillian's oldest brother, Caleb, said. "Want me and Beau to go out looking for her?"

Vince finished off his latest coffee, took a long look at Joe, then shook his head. "She'll show."

"How can you be sure?"

"Have you ever known your stubborn-streaked sister to quit a job midway through?"

EXHAUSTED, AND TERRIFIED for Joe's safety, Gillian reached her family home just before dark. The two-story, ragtag house was nestled at the base of a fern-choked ravine, the walls of which were covered in fir with trunks as big around as small countries. At the other end of the ravine raged the Pacific, cranky after the day's storms.

As a kid, she'd alternated between finding the place haunted and enchanting. Town was only a couple of miles away, yet out here, it felt as if civilization didn't exist.

Oddly enough, as much as she'd been dreading this moment, now that she'd finally accepted defeat, she looked forward to a few big hugs. To having someone else do the thinking, leaving her free to carry on with worrying.

The metallic slam of her car door echoed through the trees.

She took a deep breath. Told herself everything would be okay. The men in her family would find Joe. Once the trial was over, she'd pour out her heart to him. Nothing ventured, nothing gained. She owed it to herself to at least tell him how she felt. If he decided he still wasn't ready to pursue another relationship, that was fine. Either she'd wait or move on. At least she'd have tried.

The front porch door screeched open, and a lanky guy in need of a haircut stepped out. "You look like hell."

"Thanks," she said to Adam. "Good seeing you, too."

Handsome and self-assured as always—not to mention tall—he loped off the porch, then grabbed her around the waist and lifted her off her feet for the first of those hugs she'd been craving. "Pops said you'd come."

"He did?" Great. Was she that predictable?

"Let me get that," he said after setting her down, grabbing her briefcase and overnight bag. The rest of her belongings were back on the island. Presumably gone up in smoke.

As she trailed after Adam onto the porch, twenty years slipped away and she was once again a little girl, frowning because her brother didn't think she could carry her own science fair project home from school.

"Coming, squirt?" Holding the door open for her, he grinned.

In no mood for goofing around, she didn't.

"Yo, Pops! You'll never guess who I just found out in the front yard."

From the kitchen came a series of scrapes and metallic groans, indicative of the remaining men in her family getting up from the table.

"Hey, squirt," Beau said, ambling toward her with a welcoming smile. He snatched her into another off-her-feet hug. Then came her big brother, Caleb.

"Long time no see," he said with a faint smile. "You sure seemed in a hurry to get out of the office this morning."

She shrugged. "I had things to do. Hey, Dad." Fighting more tears, she stepped into her father's strong arms.

"Hey, princess. Sorry about your lousy day."

"Thanks."

"Funny though, how things have a way of working out."

"Not in this case," she said, voice muffled against his

chest. His red flannel shirt smelled of baked chicken. Her stomach growled.

"Sure about that?"

That dear voice…*Joe?*

Peeking out from around her father's right arm, Gillian squealed. By the time she got to the kitchen threshold, she was already in his arms, and he was lifting her. Only unlike her brothers, he urged her legs fully around his waist. She'd already flung her arms around his neck. Would she ever stop crying? "Joe, oh my God, Joe." She kissed his cheeks and chin and forehead and eyebrows and finally, his lips. Strong, beautiful, delicious lips. "What are you doing here? Never mind, I don't care why you're here, just that you are. I love you, I love you, I—"

"Ditto," he said, kissing her back and then some.

She moaned.

Behind them, her father cleared his throat. "Let's keep it clean, folks."

Reddening, she lowered her legs and Joe eased her down. But she still kept hold of his hand.

In the living room, Joe relayed the events of his day, finishing with the fact that he was flying out first thing in the morning to attend Tsun-Chung's trial.

"Vince," he said, "if it hadn't been for your daughter warning me to be careful who I trust, I'd probably be dead. This is one amazing woman you've raised."

"Tell me about it," Gillian's dad said, the smile on his face brighter than any she'd ever seen.

Joe went on and on, telling her father and brothers how they'd escaped from the island, and how she'd devised the plan to blow up the diesel generator as a diversion.

"Stop," she finally said. "I'm not the hero he makes me out to be. Bottom line, Dad, I failed you. Just like you always said, I'd be better off staying at home and raising a family."

"What?" Her father scrunched his eyebrows. "When did I ever say that?"

"I don't know. You just did. Lots of times."

"Boys? You ever recall me once saying that? Your mother would jump up from her grave to beat me over the head. In fact, on her deathbed, she made me promise to always support you in whatever you wanted to do."

"Yeah, but what about all those times you said I'd make a good mom?"

"You would. Lord knows you took care of all of us. But where did you ever get the fool idea that just because you'd make a good mom, that's the only thing I thought you'd be good at? You were a whiz at math and science. English, too. Fact is, I knew from the start you could do just about anything you set your mind to. If I— shoot, all of us—watched over you a bit too close, sorry. But after saying goodbye to your mom, I don't think a one of us could've lived through losing you, too."

Cradling her forehead in her hands, Gillian felt as if her whole adult life had been a joke. What was her father saying? That everything she'd ever believed about him had been wrong?

Joe settled his arm about her shoulders. "You guys mind if I steal a little alone time with your girl?"

"I don't know, Pops." Caleb grinned. "Think we can trust him?"

"I STILL CAN'T BELIEVE you're here," Gillian said, nestled onto her canopy bed beside Joe. The room was exactly as she'd left it on her eighteenth birthday—pink, pink and more pink. Movie posters of *Cape Fear, Bill & Ted's Bogus Journey* and *Backdraft.* High school snapshots of her and a few girlfriends she'd lost contact with hamming it up at football games. It even smelled the same—like her old perfume she used to feel so fancy wearing, White Diamonds.

And hair spray. Tons and tons of hair spray.

"It does feel weird, doesn't it?" Joe stated. "I keep thinking your dad's going to charge up here demanding we open the door."

"Shh," she said with a grin. "Don't put ideas in his head. Believe me, you're the first guy who ever made it past the stairs, let alone to my bedroom."

"I feel honored."

She felt utterly content, sinking farther into his arms. After an eternity of more kisses, she said, "Um, please don't take this the wrong way, but before tomorrow, there are a couple things I have to know."

Rolling away from her, he came close to falling off the narrow bed, but with a few more kisses and a whole lot of laughing, Gillian managed to wrangle him back to safety. "I've heard of guys getting cold feet at the serious questions," she teased, "but that was ridiculous."

His expression clouded. "That what this is, Gil? Our 'serious' talk? The one where you tell me it's been fun, but…"

"No. Oh, a thousand times no." She flattened her

palm against his chest, where his heart beat strong and steady—both qualities that at the moment she feared she lacked. "I—I just want to know," she said softly, not meeting his gaze, trying her damnedest not to cry. "Why you told my dad and brother all those lies."

"Excuse me?" All kidding aside, he sat up straight in the bed, leaning against the headboard.

"You know, about me saving you, when the whole time we've been together, you've been either saving yourself or the both of us?"

"That really how you see it?" he asked, cradling her cheek, brushing it with the pad of his thumb.

She nodded.

"Wow…" He shook his head. "I always suspected you were a little off, but…"

When he broke into a slow, sexy smile, she gave him a swat. "Joe, please. I'm serious."

"You think I'm not?" After pulling her onto his lap, he said, "You just don't get it, do you? Far more important than saving me from a few gun-toting thugs, Gillian, you saved me from living out the rest of my life alone. Mired in grief and guilt and regret." With a hand at the back of her head, he kissed her softly. "I love you. And that doesn't mean I love the memory of Willow any less, it just means I've opened my heart to love even more."

Though her own heart still trilled from the notion that this amazing man actually seemed to care for her as much as she did him, she couldn't help but ask, "How can you love me when I've been such a failure at my career?"

"Whoa," he said. "If we're going to get married— which we are—you've gotta start cutting yourself some slack. The only person in this house who sees you as a failure is you. The whole time I was sitting here, waiting for you, I got this parade of Gillian Logue show and tell. Soccer trophies, ballet pictures, science fair medals, college diploma, medals of achievement." He rolled his eyes. "I mean, after about an hour, I was glazing over from your glory, but they kept on and on. I'm telling you, they were relentless. If you hadn't shown up, saving me yet again, I might've croaked from boredom."

"Do me a favor," she said, laughing through happy tears.

"What's that?"

"Shut up and kiss me."

"Is that a yes to my proposal?"

"What proposal?"

"Weren't you listening? I said you're going to marry me."

Eyebrows raised, she said, "*That* was a proposal? Sounded more like a command."

Looking around, Joe eyed a few hair bows tacked to a nearby bulletin board. He yanked down a big red one. "Okay, woman, prepared to be dazzled."

She raised that stubborn chin of hers. Stuck out her left hand. "I'm waiting."

Fumbling with doubling over the black elastic part that was supposed to stick in her hair, he said, "Gee, thanks for the help."

"You're welcome." She winked.

Taking her hand in his, he made a mess of trying to slide the grosgrain bow onto her ring finger. "I can't believe you actually wore this monstrosity in public."

"Hey, it was the style—in third grade."

"Still…"

"Are you going to propose?"

"Well, I was thinking of asking that Heidi Klum poster down the hall in Adam's old room, but I guess you'll do."

That earned him a slug.

But then he turned serious, kissing her big red bow and the slim finger beneath it. "When we get to L.A., I'm going to buy you a rock so big you can hardly lift it, but in the meantime…Gillian Logue, will you—"

A knock sounded on the bedroom door. "Call me old-fashioned," said the booming voice of Joe's future father-in-law, "but until my little girl becomes your wife, she's still my little girl. How about keeping this door open."

Joe groaned.

Gillian pressed a quick kiss to his forehead, then hopped up from his lap to abide by her father's wishes. Once the door hung open, she asked, "There, Dad, you happy?"

"That depends," he said, crossing his arms. "You ever give this boy an answer?"

"Yeah," Joe said, joining her at the door. "I'm still waiting."

"I don't know…" Fingers to her temples, she grinned. "All this pressure. How will I ever decide?"

Her father cleared his throat. "Want me to spank her, or now that she's about to be yours, you want the honor?"

"Believe me, sir, after all she's put me through, it'd be a pleasure."

Gillian shrieked.

Joe laughed, then scooped her into his arms. "Out with it. You going to marry me?"

"You going to spank me?"

"Brother," Vince said with another shake of his head. "Knowing that stubborn streak of hers, looks like we could be here awhile. Joe, she's all yours. I'm heading back to my *TV Guide* and coffee."

Once the coast was clear, Joe pressed his lips to Gillian's, cautiously at first, but then increasing the pressure, along with the pleasure when he urged her sweet mouth open for a little tongue.

"Mmm…" she moaned. "Yes, yes."

"What was that?" he asked, setting her on her feet.

Dazed, she said, "I—I said yes to your question."

"What question? It's been so long since I asked, I kind of forgot."

"Is this what I have to look forward to for the next eighty or so years?"

Shooting her a grin, tugging her back into his arms, he said, "Yep."

"Awesome. I wouldn't want it any other way."

Epilogue

"Whoa." Joe slapped the *L.A. Times* on the tabletop.

"What?" Gillian asked, looking pretty as ever at the breakfast table of their new beachfront home. Sunlight bathed Gil and his daughter—*her* daughter—in a glow straight out of an old-world painting. Freeze-framing their images in his mind, he fell still, almost afraid to breathe for fear the moment's perfection might be a dream.

"Daddy, did you know my friend Julie Brook-something has two kittens and a dog?"

Looking as if she was trying to hide a smile, Gillian kept on brushing Meggie's long, blond hair.

He whistled. "I did not know that. Now that's some real news."

"And she has a hamster. She used to have babies and a daddy hamster, but the daddy tried to eat the babies, so her mom—she's a *vetra-er-narian*—said they should find new homes for the babies and the daddy."

"There you go, beauty queen. You're all set."

"Thanks, Gilly." Joe's heart lurched when Meghan

planted a great big, sloppy kiss on Gillian's left cheek. "You're coming today, right?"

"Wouldn't miss it."

"You're coming, too, right, Daddy?"

"I've already got it penciled in on my calendar."

"Okay, good, 'cause Grandma and Grandpa always take too many pictures, and I'd rather eat cake."

"Sure," Joe said, pulling her onto his lap to breathe her in. The scents of her shampoo and new pink dress that smelled like the mall and the grape-flavored lip gloss Gillian brought her home as a surprise from her latest out-of-town assignment. "And how many kindergarten graduations have you been to that have led you to this conclusion?"

His little girl scrunched her nose. "Huh?"

"Ignore him," Gillian said, spreading just the right amount of strawberry cream cheese on Meghan's morning bagel. Patting the little girl's chair, she said, "Come over here and eat. You don't want to be too hungry to practice walking across the gym, do you?"

"Nope," Meghan said, squirming from her dad's lap to wriggle into her chair.

On her way down, a row of sequins from her fairy wings—an added accessory that looked pretty darn cute, even if he did say so himself—scratched the underside of Joe's chin.

From outside came a sorrowful howl.

Looking very grown-up, Meghan shook her head. "Barney just doesn't learn, does he? That seagull doesn't want to be eaten."

Joe took one look at Gillian and burst out laughing.

"What's funny?" Meggie asked. "If you were a seagull, would you want Barney eating you for breakfast?"

"No, sweetie, I wouldn't," Gillian said.

"Well, me neither. Guess Daddy would." She stuck out her bagel-crusted tongue at him.

He stuck his tongue out right back.

While Meghan was busy making a mess of her breakfast, Gillian tapped the paper. "Before our kitten and hamster baby lesson, you were about to tell me something you'd read?"

"Just a reporter prophesizing about Tsun-Chung's sentencing today. Says he's expected to get three consecutive life terms."

"You sure you don't want to go?"

Joe firmly shook his head.

"Might give you closure."

He reached for his fresh-squeezed OJ. "Darlin', it's closed. I wasted two years of my life on this guy. I wouldn't waste two more seconds. I sure as hell wouldn't miss Meggie's graduation."

"That's all I wanted to know."

"Know what I want to know?" Meghan asked.

"What's that, sweetie?" Gillian wiped cream cheese smudges from the corners of the little girl's mouth.

"Whether you guys are gettin' me kittens or hamster babies for my *grat-u-lations* present. Julie says it's a special occasion, which means you have to get me something *really* good."

"Well, Gillian? You heard the girl. What shall it be, hamster babies or kitten babies?"

She turned to Meghan. "Do we have to have more than one of each?"

The little girl nodded.

"Okay, then I vote hamster babies."

"I second," Joe said. "Plus, this'll be a lot cheaper than the playhouse I was going to give you."

"A playhouse?" Her eyes got wide. "Really, Daddy? Really? Can the hamster babies live in the playhouse?"

"Absolutely."

She leaped from her chair, hurtling herself at Gillian. "Thank you, thank you. This is the best *grat-u-til-ation* ever!"

"You're welcome, sweetie."

"What about me?" Joe asked.

"Oh yeah." Meghan scrambled to him. "Thank you, too, Daddy. I love you." Coming from her, those three simple words meant the world. Tears burned in his eyes.

Those first few days after he'd come home to be a real father again had been tough. His daughter hadn't quite known what to make of him. Granted, they'd spent a few meals together when he'd been on the run, but those times had been filled with his in-laws' nervous chatter and Meggie catching him up on what all had happened in her life.

At first, she'd cried a lot for her grandparents, but after Joe assured her they were just a short car ride or phone call away, she gradually opened up to him. Asking him to read her a bedtime story or help her pick out school clothes or take her for doughnuts like he used to.

From there, the normalcy he'd so desperately craved had come tumbling back. And then Gillian had entered his and Meggie's lives. Just for short visits at first. Then family outings. Until one day when Meggie asked Gillian if she would be her second mommy. And Gillian had tearfully agreed.

Across the table, he caught Gillian staring at the two of them. Her eyes looked suspiciously wet, too.

"We've come a long way, haven't we?" He reached for her hand, giving it a squeeze. *I love you,* he mouthed. *I love you.*

From outside came more dog baying.

From inside, "Can we go get the hamster babies now?"

"What about graduation?"

"Let's skip it. I'll just do *kinder-garden* again next year. It was fun."

Fun.

Joe squeezed his wife's hand and his daughter a little harder. Yep, that perfectly summed up his new life.

* * * * *

Watch for the next book in Laura Marie Altom's U.S. Marshals series, MARRYING THE MARSHAL, coming January 2006, only from Harlequin American Romance.

Welcome to the world of American Romance!
Turn the page for excerpts
from our November 2005 titles.
CINDERELLA CHRISTMAS by Shelley Galloway
BREAKFAST WITH SANTA by Pamela Browning
HOLIDAY HOMECOMING by Mary Anne Wilson

Also, watch for a new anthology,
CHRISTMAS, TEXAS STYLE,
which features three fun and warmhearted holiday
stories by three of your favorite
Harlequin American Romance authors,
Tina Leonard, Leah Vale and Linda Warren.
Let these stories show you what it's like to celebrate
Christmas down on the ranch.

We hope you'll enjoy every one of these books!

We're thrilled to introduce a brand-new author to American Romance! Prepare yourself to be pulled in by Shelley Galloway's characters, who you'll just like. CINDERELLA CHRISTMAS *is a charming tale of a woman whose need or a particular pair of shoes starts a chain of events worthy not only of a Cinderella story, but of a fairy tale touched with the magic of Christmas.*

Oh, the shoes were on sale now. The beautiful shoes with the three gold straps, the four-inch heel and not much else. The shoes that would show off a professional pedicure and the fine arch of her foot, and would set off an ivory lace gown to perfection.

Of course, to pull off an outfit like that, she would need to have the right kind of jewelry, Brooke Anne thought as she stared at the display through the high-class shop window. Nothing too bold…perhaps a simple diamond tennis bracelet and one-carat studs? Yes, that would lend an air of sophistication. Not too dramatic, but enough to let the outfit speak for itself. Elegance. Refinement. Money.

Hmm. And an elaborate updo for her hair. Something extravagant, to set off her gray eyes and high cheekbones. Something to give herself the illusion of height she so desperately needed. It was hard to look statuesque when you were five-foot-two.

But none of that would matter when she stepped out on the dance floor. Her date would hold her tightly and twirl her around and around. She would balance on the pad of her foot as they maneuvered carefully around the floor. She would put all those dancing lessons to good use, and her date would be impressed that she could waltz with ease. They would glide through the motions, twirling, dipping, stepping together. Other dancers would stay out of their way.

No, no one would be in the way...they would have already moved aside to watch the incredible display of footwork, the vision of two bodies in perfect harmony, moving in step, gliding in precise motion. They would stare at the striking woman, wearing the most beautiful, decadent shoes...shoes that would probably only last one evening, they were so fragile.

She would look like a modern-day Mona Lisa—with blond hair and gray eyes, though. And short. She would be a short Mona Lisa. But, still graceful.

But that wouldn't matter, because she would have on the most spectacular shoes that she'd ever seen. She'd feel like...*magic.*

"May I help you?"

Brooke Anne simply stared at the slim, elegant salesman who appeared beside her. "Pardon?"

He pursed his lips, then spoke again. "Miss, do you need any help? I noticed that you've been looking in the window for a few minutes."

"No...thanks."

With a twinge of humor, Brooke Anne glanced in the window again, this time to catch the reflection staring back at her. Here she was, devoid of makeup, her hair pulled back in a hurried ponytail, dressed in old jeans and a sweatshirt that was emblazoned with Jovial Janitor Service. And her shoes…she was wearing old tennis shoes.

Pamela Browning has eaten breakfast with Santa.
It was a pancake breakfast fund-raiser for
charity, exactly like the one in her book,
and she attended dressed as Big Bird.
She thought she'd be able to relax with a
big plate of pancakes after leading the kids in songs
from "Sesame Street," but some of the
more thoughtful children had prepared her
a plate of—you guessed it—birdseed.
When she's not dressing as an eight-foot-tall bird,
Pam spends her time canoeing, taking
Latin-dance lessons and, lately,
rebuilding her hurricane-damaged house.

Bah, humbug!

The Santa suit was too short.

Tom Collyer stared in dismay at his wrists, protruding from the fur-trimmed red plush sleeves. He'd get Leanne for this someday. There was a limit to how much a big brother should do for a sister.

The pancake breakfast was the Bigbee County, Texas, event of the year for little kids, and when Leanne had asked him to participate in this year's fund-raiser for the Homemakers' Club, he hadn't taken her seriously. He was newly home from his stint in the Marine Corps, and he hadn't yet adjusted his thinking back to Texas Hill Country standards. But his brother-in-law, Leanne's husband, had come down with an untimely case of the flu, and Tom had been roped into the Santa gig.

He peered out of the closet at the one hundred kids running around the Farish Township volunteer fire department headquarters, which was where they held these blamed breakfasts every year. One of the boys was hammering another boy's head against the floor, and his mother was trying to pry them apart. A little girl with long auburn curls stood wailing in a corner.

Leanne jumped onto a low bench and clapped her hands. "Children, guess what? It's time to tell Santa Claus what you want for Christmas! Have you all been good this year?"

"Yes!" the kids shouted, except for one boy in a blue velvet suit, who screamed, "No!" A nearby Santa's helper tried to shush him, but he merely screamed "No!" again. Tom did a double take. The helper, who resembled the boy so closely that she must be his mother, had long gleaming wheat-blond hair. It swung over her cheeks when she bent to talk to the child. Tom let his gaze travel downward, and took in the high firm breasts under a clinging white sweater, the narrow waist and gently rounded hips. He was craning his neck for a better assessment of those attributes when a loudspeaker began playing "Jingle Bells." That was his cue.

After pulling his pants down to cover his ankles and plumping his pillow-enhanced stomach to better hide his rangy frame, he drew a deep breath and strode from the closet.

"Ho-ho-ho!" he said, making his deep voice even deeper. "Merry Christmas!" As directed, he headed for the elaborate throne on the platform at one end of the room.

"Santa, Santa," cried several kids.

"Okay, boys and girls, remember that you're supposed to sit at the tables and eat your breakfast," Leanne instructed. "Santa's helper elves will come to each table in turn to take you to Santa Claus. Remember to smile! An elf will take your picture when you're sitting on Santa's knee."

Tom brushed away a strand of fluffy white wig hair that was tickling his face. "Ho-ho-ho!" he boomed again in his deep faux-Santa Claus voice as he eased his unaccustomed bulk down on the throne and ceremoniously drew the first kid onto his lap. "What do you want for Christmas, little girl?"

"A brand-new candy-red PT Cruiser with a convertible top and a turbo-charged engine," she said demurely.

"A car! Isn't that wonderful! Ho-ho-ho!" he said, sliding the kid off his lap as soon as the male helper elf behind the tripod snapped a picture. Was he supposed to promise delivery of such extravagant requests? Tom had no idea.

For the next fifteen minutes or so, Tom listened as kids asked for Yu-Gi-Oh! cards, Bratz dolls, even a Learjet. He was wondering what on earth a Crash Team Bandicoot was when he started counting the minutes; only an hour or so, and he'd be out of there. "Ho-ho-ho!" he said again and again. "Merry Christmas!"

Out of the corners of his eyes, Tom spotted the kid in the blue velvet suit approaching. He scanned the crowd for the boy's gorgeous mother, who was temporarily distracted by a bottle of spilled syrup at one of the tables.

"Ho-ho-ho!" Tom chortled as a helper elf nudged the kid in the blue suit toward him. And when the kid hurled a heretofore concealed cup of orange juice into his lap, Tom's chortle became "Ho-ho-ho—oh, no!" The kid stood there, frowning. Tom shot him a dirty look and, using the handkerchief that he'd had the presence of mind to stuff into his pocket, swiped hastily at the orange rivulets gathering in his crotch. With great effort, he managed to bite back a four-letter word that drill sergeants liked to say when things weren't going well.

He jammed the handkerchief back in his pocket and hoisted the boy onto his knee. "Careful now," Tom said. "Mustn't get orange juice on that nice blue suit, ho-ho-ho!"

"Do you always laugh like that?" asked the kid, who seemed about five years old. He had a voice like a foghorn and a scowl that would do justice to Scrooge himself.

"Laugh like what?" Tom asked, realizing too late that he'd used his own voice, not Santa's.

"'Ho-ho-ho.' Nobody laughs like that." The boy was regarding him with wide blue eyes.

"Ho-ho-ho," Tom said, lapsing back into his Santa voice. "You're a funny guy, right?"

"No, I'm not. You aren't, either."

"Ahem," Santa said. "Maybe you should just tell me what you want for Christmas."

The kid glowered at him. "Guess," he said.

Tom was unprepared for this. "An Etch-a-Sketch?" he ventured. Those had been popular when he was a child.

"Nope."

"Yu-Gi-Oh! cards? A Crash Team Billy Goat…uh, I mean Bandicoot?"

"Nope."

Beads of sweat broke out on Tom's forehead. The helpers were unaware of his plight. They were busy lining up the other kids who wanted to talk to Santa.

"Yu-Gi-Oh! cards?"

"You already guessed that one." The boy's voice was full of scorn.

"A bike? Play-Doh?"

The kid jumped off his lap, disconcerting the elf with the camera. "I want a real daddy for Christmas," the boy said, and stared defiantly up at Tom....

*This is Mary Anne Wilson's third book in
her four-book miniseries entitled
RETURN TO SILVER CREEK,
the dramatic stories of four men who became
fast friends as youths in a small Nevada
town—and the unexpected turns each of
their lives has taken. Cain Stone's
tale is no exception!*

A month ago, Las Vegas, Nevada

"I'm not going back to Silver Creek," Cain Stone said. "I don't have the time, or the inclination to make the time. Besides, it's not home for me."

The man he was talking to, Jack Prescott, shook his head, then motioned with both hands at Cain's penthouse. It was done in black and white—black marble floors, white stone fireplace, white leather furniture. The only splash of color came from the sofa pillows, in various shades of red. "This is home?"

The Dream Catcher Hotel and Casino on The Strip in Las Vegas was a place to be. The place Cain worked. The part of the world that he owned. But a home? No. He'd never had one. "It's my place," he said honestly.

An angular man, dressed as usual in faded jeans, an old open-necked shirt and well-worn leather boots—despite the millions he was worth—Jack leaned back against the semi-circular couch, positioned to face the bank of windows that looked down on the sprawling city twenty stories below. "Cain, come on. You haven't been back for years, and it's the holidays."

"Bah, humbug," Cain said with a slight smile, wishing that the feeble joke would ease the growing tension in him. A tension that had started when Jack had asked him to go back to Silver Creek. "You know that for people like us there are no holidays. They're the heavy times in the year. I look forward to Christmas the way Ebenezer Scrooge did. You get through it and make as much money as you can."

Jack didn't respond with any semblance of a smile. Instead, he muttered, "God, you're cynical."

"Realistic," Cain amended with a shrug. "What I want to know, though, is why it's so important to you that I go to Silver Creek?"

"I said, it's the holidays, and that means friends. Josh is there now, and Gordie, who's in his clinic twenty-four hours a day. We can get drunk, ski down Main Street, take on Killer Run again. Whatever you want."

Jack, Josh and Gordie were as close to a family as Cain had come as a child. The orphanage hadn't been anything out of Dickens, but it hadn't been family. The three friends were. The four of them had done everything together, including getting into trouble and wiping out on Killer Run. "Tempting," Cain said, a pure lie at that moment. "But no deal."

"I won't stop asking," Jack said.

Cain stood and crossed to the built-in bar by the bank of windows. He ignored the alcohol and glasses and picked up one of several packs of unopened cards, catching a glimpse of himself in the mirrors behind the bar before he turned to Jack. He was tall, about Jack's height at six-foot-one or so, with dark hair worn a bit long like Jack's, and brushed by gray—like Jack's. His eyes, though, were deep blue, in contrast to Jack's, which were almost black.

He was sure he could match Jack dollar for dollar if he had to. And where just as Jack didn't look like the richest man in Silver Creek, Cain didn't look like a wealthy hotel/casino owner in Las Vegas. Few owners dressed in Levi's and T-shirts; even fewer went without any jewelry, including a watch. He had a closetful of expensive suits and silk shirts, but he hardly ever wore them. Still, he fit right in at the Dream Catcher Hotel and Casino. It was about the only place he'd ever felt he fit in. He didn't fit in Silver Creek. He never had.

He went back to Jack with the cards, broke the seal on the deck and said as he slipped the cards out of the package, "Let's settle this once and for all."

"I'm not going to play poker with you," Jack told him. "I don't stand a chance."

Cain eyed his friend as he sat down by him on the couch. "We'll keep it simple," he murmured. He took the cards out of the box, tossed the empty box on the onyx coffee table in front of them and shuffled the deck.

"What's at stake?" Jack asked.

"If you win, I'll head north to Silver Creek for a few days around the holidays…"